Magic Academy

Lenny Lee

INTRODUCTION

Lindsey Waters has always been a shy girl, but as a 7th grader, Lindsey was ready to try to make some friends. Trying to show everyone that she wasn't weird, Lindsey made a goal to become more social and more confident. One day as she was walking home from school contemplating a plan to get friends, Lindsey heard one of her classmates, popular and pretty student Laurie, yelling at an unknown person.

Overhearing their conversation, Lindsey learned that the two are waiting for someone to 'awaken' and save them from something. Curiosity takes over Lindsey and she decides to abandon her mission of making friends and takes on a new mission of finding out what Laurie is hiding. However, what Lindsey learned was something definitely out of a Harry Potter novel and Lindsey is ultimately the one who awakens to a world that she never thought existed.

Part one: The Awakening

Maybe I should buy some of that sweet smelling perfume. All of the favorite girls use it, and they have a lot of friends, daydreaming in class has become one of Lindsey's favorite pastimes. Being a twelve-year-old girl, Lindsey wasn't particularly famous. Lindsey kept to herself the majority of the time because she was so shy.

"Lindsey, are you listening to me?" Deep in thought, Lindsey didn't hear her teacher, Mr. Thomas, speaking to her. She could faintly make out the voices of her classmate's snickering.

I guess it is my fault, though, I don't really make an effort in speaking to anyone, looking out of the window in deep thought, Lindsey kept thinking that if she had a friend her life would be so much more interesting. Lindsey thought it wasn't natural to be a 7th grader without any friends.

"Lindsey!" Lindsey could hear the laughter getting louder, and she wished that whatever they were laughing about, they'd finish soon. She was starting to lose her train of thought. "Lindsey Waters! Are you listening to me?"

"Huh?" Lindsey blinked and looked up at the figure standing directly in front of her. The class began laughing even louder. Blushing, Lindsey finally realized that the class was laughing so hard because Mr. Thomas was speaking to her and she had been spaced out the entire time.

"What's the answer to the question that I just asked?" Mr. Thomas asked, tapping his foot quickly on the floor. Lindsey's face burned with embarrassment, and she could feel tears threatening to spill from her eyes.

"I don't know," Lindsey's voice was low, and her discomfort was present in it.

"And why is that, Ms. Waters?" Lindsey knew that she should have been listening to Mr. Thomas' lesson and not daydreaming, but that didn't give him the right to embarrass her.

"Because I wasn't listening," the class was hollering in amusement.

"She's so weird," one favorite girl named Laurie said.

"Yeah, that's why I don't talk to her. I'm afraid that some of her oddness will rub off on me."

"She's always daydreaming, no wonder she's constantly asking questions," the class continued to make fun of Lindsey and Lindsey lowered her eyes so that she was looking at her desk and not at the other students.

"Pay more attention, Lindsey," Mr. Thomas said, walking away. "Everybody be quiet. I hear you over there snickering. Just remember that some of you aren't even earning a decent grade in my class. You have no right to talk about anyone else just because they lost track of the lesson." The students grew silent then, and Lindsey smiled to herself.

I'm not the most outgoing student in the room, but I am one of the smartest. Now and then Lindsey drifted off into her own world and continuously had to ask questions because she wasn't paying attention. But at the end of the day, she kept her grades up.

"Humph!" Laurie said, and Lindsey looked up at the fairly pretty girl. Her rosy cheeks, long flowing hair, and fair skin, there was no wonder why Laurie was famous and had so many friends. Lindsey wasn't bad looking; she felt that she was a bit on the plain side. Freckles covered her tan skin, and her medium dark hair was unruly, but she didn't consider herself unlikable because of her looks.

Laurie continued staring angrily at Lindsey before she turned around and resumed listening to Mr. Thomas' lecture. What did I do to upset her that much? Lindsey thought to herself. If Laurie was mad at Mr. Thomas' comment, she should be giving him the evil eye and not Lindsey.

"Lindsey!" jumping in fright, Lindsey's eyes went towards the front of the class where Mr. Thomas was staring right at her!

"What did we just discuss?"

"Uh… to pay attention to the lesson," Lindsey said as another blush tinted her cheeks crimson. The classroom snickered again, but this time, they controlled themselves when Mr. Thomas glared at each and every one of the laughing students.

"Right, so stop daydreaming and focus!" Nodding her head quickly, Lindsey picked up her pen and began taking notes.

*****

After class had ended, Lindsey made her way towards her locker to get her jacket and the few books that she needed for the day. Since she was out of class, Lindsey could finish thinking about how to gain more confidence so that she could make some friends.

"Maybe I should invite a few of the girls over to my place for a sleepover," Lindsey's mom was an excellent cook, and Lindsey was sure that her mother wouldn't mind. "But who should I ask, though?" The majority of all the girls stayed away from her, but there was one girl, Eliza, who always said hello to Lindsey in the morning.

Eliza was a sweet young lady and equally as shy as Lindsey. Eliza was the shortest in the class, and she had a voice so high pitched that if mice could talk, Lindsey was sure that their voice would be as squeaky and adorable as Eliza's. The problem was that even though Eliza says hello to Lindsey that was the only words that she shared with Eliza.

"Maybe she doesn't know what to say?" A few students looked at Lindsey as she headed out of the door, probably wondering why she was talking to herself. When Lindsey noticed the curious glances, she got embarrassed that she had gotten caught talking to herself. Stop talking to yourself out loud! It was bad enough that everyone already thought she was weird.

Walking down the street instead of taking the school bus, she had decided earlier that year to avoid the school bus at all times when it's possible. Even though she wanted friends, she felt awkward on the school bus. No one sat next to her, and she didn't have anyone to speak with during those long thirty minutes.

"This is going to be a long year if I don't have friends." Next year she'd be ready to graduate, and she didn't want to go to high school friendless. "Then again, I could start over." The girls on the television show that Lindsey watched were the 'rejects' in one school and then favorite in the next. "But I want to start over fresh now!"

"Her? You had a vision of her? That girl is a nutcase!" Stopping in her tracks, Lindsey was brought out of her thoughts by a screaming voice. It wasn't the screaming that made Lindsey end; it was the screamer's voice.

"I've heard that voice before." Poking her head around the corner of an abandoned building, Lindsey was surprised to see Laurie speaking to someone who Lindsey wasn't able to see. Why is Laurie behind an abandoned building, that isn't safe! Generally, Lindsey would have minded her own business and kept walking, but she decided to stay there just in case something went wrong.

"Listen, you might not be fond of the young girl, but it won't stop the fact that she'll become one of us. As soon as this happens, you'll need to train her so that she could help us defeat it," What and who are they talking about and what will this person become? What are they trying to beat?

"She's so weird, how would she be of any help to us? I tell you that we'd have a better chance of getting a poodle to help. I'm telling you now that I won't have anything to do with her." Laurie pushed her straight hair out of her face then.

"You say that now but when the time comes, you two will be the best of friends." Before Laurie had enough time to deny the mystery person's comment, a thick layer of purple smoke engulfed the air around Laurie.

Lindsey's eyes grew wide in horror and amazement when the smoke cloud disappeared, and Laurie and the person she was speaking with were gone.

2

"Mom…Mom!" Lindsey cried out running through the house like she had just seen a ghost.

"Quiet down Lindsey. I'm in the kitchen," Running towards the kitchen, Lindsey saw her mother, Amy Waters, standing by the stove.

"You're not going to believe what I just saw! Laurie from my class was talking to some mysterious person about helping some weird girl defeat something, and out of nowhere a cloud of purple smoke went poof, and they were gone." Amy blinked her eyes a few times trying to decipher the blabbering that escaped from her daughter's lips.

"That is some images that you have dear."

"Mom, I didn't imagine it. I saw it with my own two eyes," Lindsey said. She might have lost her sense of reality sometimes, but this time, she was sure of what she had seen.

"Maybe you did see something, but I'm pretty sure there's a logical explanation for that dear. Now sit down and eat your lunch." Sighing, Lindsey sat down at the table. She was absolutely confident that something fishy was going on. She didn't believe in magicians, there's always a trick to their 'powers,' but Lindsey still couldn't explain what she had just seen.

"I guess I can ask Laurie about it tomorrow," she doubted that the girl would tell her. Laurie probably wouldn't even acknowledge her when she asks.

"Were they out in the open?" Amy asked, and Lindsey shook her head in shame.

"No, I heard Laurie yelling and found her behind an abandoned building. She… they didn't even know I was there." Amy looked at Lindsey displeased.

"Now you know you shouldn't have been eavesdropping. I didn't raise you to be that way." Lindsey didn't need for her mother to tell her what she had done was wrong because she knew that already.

"I know me, it's just that when I heard Laurie scream, I had to make sure that she was okay. I don't know why I stood there and listened. It was almost like I was meant to be there." Placing Lindsey's lunch on the table, her mother took off her apron.

"Well when you saw that she was alright, you should have left them alone." Bending down to kiss Lindsey on her forehead, she made her way out of the kitchen. "Your father is sleeping, he had to work late all night. So it'll be best if you are quiet as a mouse." Richard Waters, Lindsey's father, was a doctor and his job kept him up all hours of the day and night. There was no wonder why he was fast asleep already.

"Fine," Lindsey said and ate her hamburger in silence. There is definitely something fishy about what I saw today, even if mom says that there's a perfectly good logical reason for it, Lindsey thought as she picked the pickles off of her burger and ate them separately. I mean, who just vanishes in purple smoke? That just doesn't happen in real life. Plus, even if it was a trick I would have at the very least seen evidence of them walking away. For a twelve-year-old girl, Lindsey was sharp when it came to observing things.

After eating her lunch, Lindsey got up and grabbed her book bag. Even though many thoughts ran through her mind, she still needed to get her homework done for tomorrow. It seemed like a long shot, but she'd ask Laurie about what she saw at school tomorrow.

*****

She hasn't looked my way once, Lindsey thought as Laurie faced the front of the classroom. Typically Laurie would look around and speak to some of her friends, but today she kept her attention on Mr. Thomas. Lindsey looked towards the front of the class every so often to keep Mr. Thomas from yelling at her like he did yesterday.

How should I do this? After promising herself that she would talk to Laurie today, she didn't take into consideration how socially awkward she is. I honestly don't know why I considered asking her, she might get mad at me for listening in on a, I guess, meaningful conversation.

"Lindsey," looking at the front of the classroom quickly,

Lindsey saw Mr. Thomas' eyes focused on her. "Were you drifting off again?" She was, but she was too embarrassed to admit that she had made the same mistake two days in a row.

"No, I heard everything that you said," that wasn't completely a lie, she did hear some of what Mr. Thomas said.

"Oh, is that so? Well, what was the question that I asked the class?" Thinking quickly, Lindsey searched her brain to see what she remembered hearing him say.

"What branch is the United States President the head of?"

"And?" Mr. Thomas asked expecting an answer. Lindsey was just excited that she had heard enough of what he was talking about to answer his question.

"The President of the United States is the head of the Executive branch." Without looking at Lindsey, Mr. Thomas began giving the lesson again. Thankfully I knew the answer. Briefly looking at the class, Lindsey noticed that there were a few students who had their eyes on her. They were probably expecting Lindsey to mess up, so she was happy to know that she wouldn't give them the satisfaction.

"Humph," looking towards the window, Lindsey saw Laurie's angry and piercing eyes glaring at her before Laurie returned her gaze towards the front of the class. Lindsey really wanted to get to the bottom of what she had seen, and maybe she'd have the courage to ask Laurie what she did to cause this apparent dislike for her.

As soon as class ended, Lindsey took in a deep breath and walked over to Laurie, who was talking to several other girls.

"I might go to the mall today. I've had this purse for a month too long, and it's time for an upgrade." Swinging her long straight hair over her shoulder, the other students appeared to be mesmerized by Laurie. One day soon people will want to hear me talk as well, Lindsey thought as she stopped in front of the girls. They stopped talking and looked at Lindsey.

"Well look what the wind blew in," one of the girls said, and the whole group began laughing. Lindsey never actually spoke to anyone in the class, so it took her a while to say what she needed to say.

"H… Hi Laurie," Blushing, Lindsey was mad at herself for not being able to keep the tremble out of her voice.

"Lindsey," Laurie said unimpressed that Lindsey had interrupted their conversation. Placing her hands on her hips, she eyed the young socially awkward girl. "What do you want?"

"Don't talk to her Laurie, she's weird." One of Laurie's friends whispered. Laurie didn't appear to have heard them because her eyes were still planted on Lindsey's.

"I have something to ask you, and I'd rather not do it

here," Lindsey said, finally able to tell what she needed to say. Her cheeks stayed a dark shade of crimson. Laurie didn't mainly look like she wanted to have a conversation with Lindsey, but she looked as if she was considering it.

"I'll talk to you later," Laurie said telling her friends goodbye. She picked up her book bag and purse before looking at Lindsey again. "Let's go and don't keep me too long." Lindsey was actually surprised that Laurie had agreed to speak with her.

Lindsey followed behind Laurie clumsily as Laurie led them through the building. For a moment there, Lindsey started to feel like she was walking around the school with a friend. Laurie wasn't the person that Lindsey thought would open her arms to call her a friend, but it was nice for Lindsey to pretend this was the case.

"Alright, let's go in here," opening the door to an empty classroom, the two of them entered, and Laurie closed the door behind them. "So what do you want?" Laurie asked, getting straight to business. Lindsey was nervous, how should I ask her this?

"I… I don't talk to people often so I'll just spit out what I'm trying to say." Deep breath, you can do this Lindsey. "I saw you speaking to someone behind a building yesterday, and I was wondering exactly how did you two disappear in a cloud of purple smoke like that?" Laurie's eyes went wide, and Lindsey immediately regretted asking Laurie that question.

3

Laurie looked at Lindsey and Lindsey looked at Laurie, neither one speaking. The shock that initially spread across Laurie's face told Lindsey that her question would have consequences. Please just say something! Almost like Laurie had read Lindsey's mind, she exploded in anger.

"You were spying on me?" Jumping back at the sudden aggressiveness from Laurie, Lindsey shook her head quickly.

"No, it's nothing like that," Lindsey started explaining. "I was walking by, and I heard you yelling. I was trying to make sure that you were alright and I caught a bit of your conversation. I didn't mean to listen. Just when I was about to walk away, the two of you disappeared." Laurie didn't seem pleased with Lindsey's explanation.

"Look, what you saw... just forget about it and never ask me about it again. That was a private moment, and you invaded my privacy." Blushing, Lindsey looked away ashamed. Her mother was right; she shouldn't have brought it up because she had offended the girl. After looking at Lindsey angrily for a few more moments, Laurie exited the classroom.

"What did I just do?" Lindsey asked herself. She only wanted to know how they were able to disappear like that. Other than her mother, Lindsey wasn't going to tell anyone else about what she saw. Lindsey knew that if Laurie wanted that information out, she wouldn't have hidden from the view of possible onlookers.

"Well, that's one person that I know will never be my friend." Lindsey was proud of herself for being able to speak to someone, but she had chosen the wrong topic to discuss. Sighing while trying to compose herself, Lindsey walked out of the classroom and hustled towards the front of the building.

"That was incredibly awkward," Lindsey mumbled to herself once she was outside. She knew that this would be another reason why people would think she was weird. "Then again, Laurie made it seem like it was a secret or something like that." After thinking about the situation a little more, Lindsey was sure that Laurie wouldn't tell anyone what had happened.

Lindsey decided to go straight home and refuse to stop if she heard random yelling or saw something odd. She didn't want a repeat of what had just happened.

"When are you going to take the bus home, Lindsey?" Lindsey's mother asked as soon as Lindsey walked into the house.

"Mom, I told you already that I don't like the bus."

"I'll feel better with you taking the bus home instead of walking home by yourself sweetheart." Lindsey knew that her mother was just worried about her, but she was okay with walking home. It's the only exercise that she'd get. She was too shy and uncoordinated to try out for the cheer team, and she was too clumsy to run track.

"Mom, please don't make me take the bus. I feel so awkward on the bus, and I don't have anyone to talk to." Amy knew that her daughter wasn't the type to socialize with others even though she couldn't stop talking when she was at home.

"Alright Lindsey, I might have to borrow your dad's car sometimes so that I can take you, or I can walk with you some of the ways." Lindsey thought that was a bad idea. Not only will people make fun of her for being 'weird,' but they'd also call her a baby.

"I'm twelve years old, not a little kid," Lindsey said stubbornly, and her mother smiled.

"Okay, maybe I won't walk you then, but I could drive you some time." Lindsey liked that idea better. Standing on her tiptoes, Lindsey kissed her mother on the cheek and made her way towards her bedroom.

"I'm going to do my homework, I'll be out later," With that said, Lindsey closed her bedroom door behind her and got started on her work.

*****

"She is definitely the one," Lindsey tried to open her eyes to see who was talking, but she couldn't. Lindsey couldn't move. She couldn't speak. The only thing she could do was listen. Is this a dream? Lindsey thought to herself because she knew that this couldn't possibly be the reality. But why do the voices sound so… real?

"She's not much now, but she will be the one to save us all. Who would have thought our savior would be a twelve-year-old girl?" What are they talking about? Who's going to save them? What is this person going to protect these people from?

"Humph! I don't care what you say, I will never accept her!" Lindsey knew that voice, but for some odd reason, she couldn't put a name to the sound. I've surely heard this voice before. Hundreds of times!

"Hush now sister. Whether you like it or not, she will become one of us, and she will be our sister. We all will aid our savior in any way that we can to assist us."

"Whatever! I'm leaving. Unlike you two I have school tomorrow," after a moment or two, the voice that Lindsey recognized was gone.

"We should get going as well sister, we've been in her mind for too long, I'm sure she's puzzled by everything that's being said." Did these people know that Lindsey could hear them?

"Yes, we don't want her to fall behind in school because her mind ran wild all night." The voice chuckled and then all of a sudden the sounds were gone. Lindsey still couldn't move or speak, but finally, her restless consciousness allowed her to fall asleep.

The next morning Lindsey woke up thinking that something odd had happened last night, but she couldn't remember what.

"Why can't I remember it?" Lindsey asked walking into the kitchen so that she could eat a bowl of cereal before she left. After struggling to try to remember what it was that she forgot, she finally gave up. "If I can't remember it then it must have not been too important." Wolfing down her breakfast, Lindsey told her mother goodbye.

"Have a good day at school, sweetheart," Amy said, and Lindsey was out of the door. It was a bit chilly outside, and Lindsey started to question this whole, walking to and from school to avoid being lonely and feeling awkward on the bus.

"Then again, what's a better way to make friends if not on the school bus?" Lindsey entertained possibly riding on the bus and forcing herself to talk to the other students, but stopped when she saw a small silhouette blocking her path. "Excuse me," Lindsey said and stood rigid when she saw that Laurie was the one in front of her.

"I'm going to tell you this one time," Laurie said and flipped her hair over her shoulder. Lindsey didn't understand why Laurie was outside walking when she usually got a ride to school. Was Laurie waiting for Lindsey by any chance?

"W… what are you doing out here?" Lindsey asked. Laurie closed the distance between them and was so close to Lindsey that she could smell the Double Mint gum that she was chewing.

"We will never be friends. I will never acknowledge you as a sister, and you will never be our savior!" Laurie screamed this at Lindsey and Lindsey stood there confused. What is she talking about? Turning on her heels, Laurie stormed off towards the direction of the school leaving Lindsey dumbfounded and all of a sudden it hit her.

"This has something to do with that dream I had last night!"

4

All night Lindsey tossed and turned and had odd dreams of fighting alongside Laurie. She couldn't see what they were fighting, or at least, she couldn't remember exactly what it was that they were fighting. When she woke up on Saturday morning, instead of watching her favorite shows that frequently broadcasted on Saturdays, Lindsey was deep in thought.

"Whatever is going on with Laurie, it's definitely not something that is normal," No matter what angle Lindsey viewed the situation in, she could not think of any logical explanation.

"Not watching your cartoons today?" Amy asked, walking into the kitchen surprised to see her daughter at the table and not in front of the television.

"No, I have too much on my mind."

"What could keep a twelve-year-old girl from the TV on her day off?" Amy asked curiously. Lindsey never missed her shows on purpose. Something had to be up with her. Lindsey knew that her mother wouldn't want to know that Lindsey was still stuck on Laurie, so she decided to tell her mother about the test that her class has on Monday.

"Oh, my class is taking a test in science on Monday. My teacher did a review of what's going to be on it, and I'm guessing this test is going to be super hard. His tests are never easy, and I know it's going to cause me some problems." Lindsey's answer was safe even though she knew that the test hadn't even crossed her mind.

"Hmmm… are you sure that's on your mind? You usually don't worry too much about those types of things." Lindsey always did her homework and kept up with her studies fairly well, so it was hard to believe that a test was worrying her. Lindsey bit her bottom lip as she thought about what she'd say next.

I was not expecting her to say that Lindsey thought. Maybe the whole test thing wasn't a good cover up considering how high her grades are. "Yes mom," she said sticking with her story. "I know I pass all of my tests because I study and do my homework, but I have trouble too." Amy looked at her daughter for a little while longer before nodding her head.

"Okay sweetheart, but don't stress too much about it. Study this weekend and ask your father or me for help if you need some." Turning towards the refrigerator, Amy started to prepare breakfast. "I'm sure you'll do well Lindsey. You're a brilliant young girl." Smiling at her mother's compliment, Lindsey stood up.

"Thanks, mom," she turned to make her way out of the kitchen and paused momentarily. "Can I ask you a question, mom?" Lindsey asked her mother hesitantly.

"Sure, what's on your mind?" Blushing in embarrassment, Lindsey felt a little silly about the question she was about to ask, but she had to know.

"Do you believe in magic? Like real magic, not those illusions magicians do." Turning to look at her daughter, Amy thought about Lindsey's question for a while.

"I believe there is magic in anyone if they actually put their minds to it. What kind of magic are you talking about?" Lindsey really just wanted her mother to say yes or no. She didn't want to look like a baby saying magic as far as wizards.

"No not that type of magic. I mean the sort of magic that Harry Potter uses," Lindsey blushed deeply in embarrassment. She thought her mother would laugh at her or look at her like she was crazy. Lindsey was surprised when her mother looked at her seriously.

"Is this a trick question?" Amy asked raising her eyebrow, and Lindsey shook her head.

"No! Please, Mom, give me your honest answer."

"No, Lindsey. Harry Potter is just a fictional character and the things he is able to do are not real." Lindsey knew that her question was silly, and she thought she was silly for even considering it, but that was the only explanation that she could come up with.

"Thanks, mom," leaving the kitchen quickly, Lindsey went back to her bedroom.

*****

Lindsey put off thinking about Laurie for the rest of Saturday and all of Sunday. Even though Lindsey knew she'd do fine, she used that time to study for her test on Monday. Lindsey walked into her class Monday afternoon confident that she'd pass her test with flying colors and she was sure that she had because she flew through the questions.

"Finally!" a student called out once the last bell of the day rang.

"Justin, do not be yelling out like that in class. The bell doesn't release you, I do!" The teacher called out angrily. Justin flinched.

"So... sorry," Justin mumbled. Lindsey wasn't paying attention to the small commotion that was going on in the class, Lindsey's focus was on one thing or one person in particular. Laurie! The girl hadn't said anything to any of her friends today no matter how many times they tried to get her attention.

Something's wrong with her, Lindsey thought. Does it have something to do with what she said to me last week? Laurie was acting strange, and Lindsey was dying to know why. Lindsey's primary focus these last few weeks was about getting enough courage to make friends. She had completely disregarded that now, her new goal was to find out Laurie's secret!

Something's drawing me to her, and I must find out! Lindsey started putting her things away quickly once her teacher dismissed them. She kept her eyes on Laurie because Lindsey felt a strong need to follow her. The way that Laurie quickly put her things away and made it to the door without speaking or even looking at her friends was suspicious of her. As soon as Laurie walked out of the door, Lindsey took off after her. Lindsey knew that she must have appeared strange to her classmates, but she didn't care. I must catch her!

Lindsey could barely keep Laurie in her line of view long enough. Lindsey needed to follow her, but it wasn't like she wanted to be caught running after her. How would Lindsey explain that to the other girl? When she made it outside, Lindsey had a real hard time keeping up with Laurie then because Laurie broke into a run.

"What is she doing?" Lindsey asked herself and started running after Laurie. She was beginning to get a little worried that she might be over her head with the mystery behind Laurie. The other girl wasn't acting like herself, and Lindsey knew if Laurie's friends saw the girl at that moment, they'd be suspicious of her behavior as well.

After several long minutes of running, Lindsey followed Laurie to an abandoned playground. The grass and the trees were high, and this definitely wasn't the place for a popular girl to be. However, the grassy plain gave Lindsey the advantage of being able to hide.

"Cir! Cir!" Laurie cried out. Lindsey crouched low and followed behind Laurie curiously. Please don't catch me now. If anyone sees me like this, there is no talking myself out of spying on Laurie. "Cir!" Who is this 'Cir' person? Lindsey thought to herself. Right as Lindsey thought that, she saw a familiar purple glow.

"It's about time that you've come, sister." Lindsey could barely stifle the gasp that escaped from her lips when a person came out of the purple smoke.

5

"Cir, how did this happen? I thought the other sisters were guarding the portal? It shouldn't have been able to get through!" Laurie yelled at the being known as Cir. Lindsey couldn't believe her eyes. Cir's hair was so light that it almost looked white and it flowed beautifully around her slender body. Lindsey couldn't tell how old the girl was, her hair and face did not match each other. Cir's face looked almost like a porcelain doll, and her hair was lighter than Lindsey's grandma's.

"Pretty..." Lindsey said in awe, but she quickly brought her attention back to the situation at hand.

"The other sisters were attacked by something that Chaos created," Cir said.

"Chaos! Did Chaos get in as well?" Laurie asked in horror. Chaos? Do they mean Chaos like destruction? Lindsey could barely make out Cir shaking her head.

"No, he's still trapped behind the portal, but his power is growing. The fact that those... things actually were able to come through the portal," Cir paused shaking her head. "He's powerful, sister. He's even been interfering with all that I can see. I can't see what the future holds for us or his plans clearly anymore."

"What do we do? We're running out of time!"

"We must wait for her to awaken. She's our only hope." Laurie made a face of disgust when Cir said that. Who are they waiting for? "I must leave now, sister. I have to help the others. There may be more of them seeping through." Without waiting for Laurie to respond, a cloud of purple smoke engulfed Cir, and she was gone.

"Why does it have to be her? A weird girl like her will be the savior of our kind? I don't care how much of a psychic Cir is. She has to be wrong!" Walking in the grass in Lindsey's direction, Lindsey froze. If she moved, she'd be seen, and if Lindsey remained where she was at, Laurie would run into her.

Should I just tell her that I'm here? Just when Lindsey thought her cover was about to be blown, Laurie stopped a few inches from Lindsey. Laurie was so close to Lindsey that she was able to smell the scent of her perfume! Lindsey feared if she breathed the wrong way she'd be discovered.

"The present is now, but the future is where I need to be.

Through the poor and the rich neighborhoods, winds guide me!

My powers are strong and able to soar me through the sky.

Take me home to my room: body, soul, and mind!"

Is she chanting a spell? Lindsey thought to herself. She's seen many shows about magic, witches, and wizards, so she knew a spell when she heard it. Her eyes grew wide at this. She chose to ignore the hints that magic might have been involved with this because it sounded just too crazy. But as she watched Laurie chant a spell, she couldn't just push this to the side and say that magic didn't exist. One moment Laurie was there, the next moment she disappeared leaving a gust of the wind in her departure.

"I can't believe that I'm saying this, but I think Laurie is a witch," Lindsey said, standing to her feet.

*****

Lindsey didn't tell her mother about what she had seen that day because she knew that her mother wouldn't believe her. Plus, it wasn't Lindsey's secret to tell anyone what she had seen. However, knowing that Laurie is a witch was incredible, and Lindsey wanted to get to know the girl better. Lindsey was a big fan of Harry Potter so to learn that witches and wizards were real changed Lindsey's world.

"It's decided. Laurie and I will become friends." Lindsey said to herself in the girls' bathroom at school the next day. Lindsey wasn't able to focus on anything that day but Laurie. When Lindsey got to school that day, she was sad to see Laurie wasn't there, but that didn't stop Lindsey from making a plan to become closer to the girl.

"It'll be tough, but I think despite all of our differences, we can become great friends." Lindsey thought that maybe she could help Laurie in some way with the problems she is going through. "What she was talking about with Cir sounded pretty serious. Something created by Chaos has come from out of a portal that they were guarding. This Chaos person must be strong."

Lindsey spent too much time in the bathroom, and it was almost time for her class to end. She made her way to her class and daydreamed for the last ten minutes. The final bell chimed, and Lindsey was up and out of her seat before the other students had even packed up their belongings.

"Today was a complete waste," Lindsey mumbled and made her way outside. She wanted desperately to speak to Laurie again today so that she could get on her right side. Lindsey knew that her shyness and the fact that she was socially awkward would get in her way, but she was still going to try.

"I'll try again tomorrow," Lindsey said sadly and made her journey home. She walked that familiar route home and stopped walking when she was five minutes away from her house. "I'm too depressed to go back, and I know mom will ask me questions." Lindsey did not feel like explaining to her mother why she was so sad, so she decided to cool down a little before going home.

"I'll just go to the park for a little while; I'm sure that mom won't mind me being a few minutes late." Turning on her heels, Lindsey made her way in the direction of the park with her head hung low. "Maybe she was sick today. Maybe she got a cold from traveling through Heaven knows what to get home yesterday." Lindsey thought of many scenarios as to why Laurie wasn't at school today. As Lindsey walked towards a bench in the deserted park, she almost screamed when a loud voice interrupted her thoughts.

"How were you able to escape from the portal?!"

"Laurie?!" Lindsey's head snapped towards the direction of Laurie's voice. It was Laurie, and there was somebody else there with her.

"Ha! Do you think those low-level witches would be able to hold me back? They're weak and so are you. Chaos will take over this pathetic world and I, Serenity will be this world's princess." The girl wearing all red with matching fiery hair blew fire onto her fingers and shot it in Laurie's direction.

"Ah!" Laurie said barely able to dodge the fireball. Lindsey's eyes went wide in pure horror.

"Oh my God, they are fighting, in the middle of the day, with magic!" Lindsey couldn't believe what she was seeing, and she couldn't think that the two girls hadn't noticed her presence.

"Electric Storm!" Laurie screamed, and electricity started shooting from her fingertips. Serenity dodged

Laurie's attack with ease and quickly countered it with another fireball which hit Laurie with excellent precision. "Ah!" Laurie cried out again as she landed on the ground.

"Like I said, pathetic." The other girl said and began walking towards Laurie, grinning. From Lindsey's viewpoint, she could tell that Laurie was afraid.

"I must help her!" Lindsey was not the strong type, but she didn't like the look in Serenity's eyes. Looking around quickly, Lindsey spotted a rather large stick and ran over to it and grabbed it. "Hah!" Lindsey cried out and ran over towards the two girls. Serenity looked back over her shoulder quickly, but not quick enough before Lindsey hit the girl with the stick and jumped on her back.

"What the? Unhand me human!" Serenity yelled and gripped Lindsey's arms in a vise grip.

"No, I won't let you hurt Laurie!" The usually quiet and shy girl was brave and confident. Lindsey's heart was in a good place as she tried to protect Laurie, but she was not a match for the witch. Serenity managed to pry Lindsey's fingers from around her and threw her to the ground in front of Laurie.

"Pathetic," Serenity said and blew fire onto her fingers and smiled maniacally at Lindsey. "If this witch was no match for me, what makes you think a mere human would be?" Shaking her head and laughing, "It's going to be too fun taking over this world." With one final snicker, she aimed her magic at Lindsey.

"No!" Laurie screamed and jumped to her feet. "Electric Storm!" she shouted and shot her magic at the evil witch. The smile didn't leave Serenity's face as she quickly pointed her fingers at Laurie shooting the powerful fireball at her.

"No, you'll hurt each other!" Lindsey screamed and jumped up in front of the spells, and instead of hitting Laurie or Serenity, it hit Lindsey.

"Lindsey!" Laurie screamed out in horror, but Lindsey couldn't hear her as her body hit the ground hard.

6

"Lindsey!" Laurie screamed again and ran over to the fallen girl.

"Ha! Ha! Ha! That was too perfect." Serenity snickered. "And this is the world that your group wants to protect? A world of weak and defenseless humans. Join us, Laurie. Chaos would show you the world that is meant for witches" Laurie didn't listen to Serenity as she shook Lindsey in an attempt to wake her.

"Ugh, I'm fine. That fireball hurts," Lindsey groaned and lifted her face up to meet Laurie's and when she did Laurie gasped.

"The seal of the sisterhood!" Lindsey looked at Laurie in confusion.

"The seal of the what?" Lindsey asked still feeling a bit clumsy from Serenity's attack. Laurie stood up and turned towards Serenity.

"This girl is not some mere human. This girl is a witch from the sisterhood and she is the destined one to destroy Chaos!" Laurie said, and for a moment, Serenity's eyes widened.

"Oh? Is this the one your pathetic lot's Cir foretold will destroy Chaos?" Serenity looked at Lindsey, and Lindsey's mouth kept opening and closing lost for words. What did Serenity and Laurie just say? I'm the destined one to destroy Chaos?

"Yes, and even though she is a new member, we still have enough power here and now to take you back to headquarters to be questioned." Lindsey didn't know what Laurie was talking about, but she knew for a fact that she wouldn't be able to provide much assistance to Laurie in her current state. Serenity looked at Lindsey and Laurie and sighed.

"I have to report this information to Chaos, but don't worry, I'll be back to finish what we started."

"Wait!" Laurie shouted and ran towards Serenity, but she was too late. In mere seconds fire engulfed Serenity's body and she was gone. "Tsk!" Laurie hissed angrily and turned towards Lindsey. "Are you sure you're alright?" For the first time since they'd known each other, Laurie finally looked at Lindsey seriously.

"Yes... but what's going on?"

"No time to explain, we must go to headquarters, and we must speak with Cir." Grabbing Lindsey's arm, Laurie began chattering.

"The time has come to present our savior.

The time is now, here in the present not later.

Let's go to a place she can meet her supporters.

Transport us now to the sisterhood's headquarters!"

"Hah!" Lindsey screamed as the world around her disappeared. Fluorescent colors appeared in her line of vision, and she couldn't think straight, but she did feel a gentle arm wrapping around her. She knew that the person guiding her through this path of colors was Laurie and when Lindsey tried to speak, her words would not come.

Finally, after what seemed like hours, the colors disappeared, and they were in an all-white room.

"You've finally arrived." A voice called out, and Cir appeared in front of Lindsey and Laurie. "So our savior has come? It's nice to meet you, sister." Cir said and approached Lindsey. Lindsey had to blink several times to clear her vision.

"What do you mean savior? Why is everyone calling me that?" Sighing, Laurie released Lindsey's arm and walked over to Cir.

"This one jumped between Serenity and my fight. That's how she became a witch. That blast should have eliminated her, but the only thing she experienced was minor pains." Laurie said shaking her head in disbelief. "I hate to admit this, but she is stronger than I initially gave her credit for." Lindsey's cheeks reddened at that.

"Hey! Can one of you answer my question?" This was the most that Lindsey has ever spoken to someone since starting middle school, and she was shocked that she was able to talk to them without her voice shaking.

"Yes, follow me, sister. I would like you to meet the others, and then we'll explain the situation to you." With a snap of her fingers; Laurie, Lindsey, and Cir disappeared in a cloud of purple smoke.

*****

Meeting the witches at the sisterhood's headquarters was overwhelming, but for the first time in Lindsey's life, she felt right at home. Lindsey was nervous speaking to so many people, but everyone was kind to her and answered all of her questions.

"So this Chaos person, is he such a threat to Earth?" Lindsey asked. They told her about the prophecy of a young girl saving the witches and humans from Chao's evil intent, and Cir told Lindsey that she knew that Lindsey would be the one that would save them since she'd been a young girl. Being a psychic has its advantages, Cir told Lindsey.

"Yes, he is building an army of evil witches and creating monstrosities to overtake the Earth. We need your help in securing the future for good witches and all of humanity." Cir walked over to Lindsey and took both of her hands in hers. "Please Lindsey, join us in our cause to protect the world and the future of our kind."

Lindsey looked around the enormous room filled with witches, some old and some young. Lindsey looked at Laurie who had her eyes on everything but Lindsey.

Lindsey could tell that the other girl didn't want her to be there, but Laurie didn't voice her opinions for Lindsey to know that as a fact. Lindsey took in a deep breath and nodded her head slowly.

"Of... of course. I'd love to do whatever I can to help." This was so surreal to Lindsey that she almost felt that she was dreaming.

"Sister Lindsey said yes, did you hear that sisters? We're saved!" The witches started cheering for Lindsey and Lindsey couldn't help the wide grin that spread across her face. Lindsey felt needed; she felt like she had friends, and Lindsey felt loved. Sighing, Laurie finally turned to Lindsey and grabbed her arm.

"It's too loud in here. Come with me," Laurie didn't give Lindsey enough time to say yes or to say no. As the two of them walked down a long corridor, a thought went across Lindsey's mind.

"What time is it? I was supposed to be at home!" Lindsey said once she realized that it's been a long time since she left school.

"Don't worry. Cir predicted that I would bring you here today. She's created an illusion spell to make your mother think that you're at home already." Lindsey was impressed; she didn't know that the witches were able to do that. Stopping abruptly, Laurie turned to Lindsey.

"Look, I think you're weird, and I do not particularly like you," Lindsey hid her head in embarrassment. She couldn't believe that Laurie up and said that to her. "But you are one of us, and I have to treat you like one of us."

"Okay?" Lindsey wasn't sure exactly sure where Laurie was going with this.

"This is not some fantasy that you've read in books or seen on TV. What is happening is the reality, and this is a reality that we must protect. If we fail; the world will be overrun by evil. You are the key to saving us all, and I want you to know that this isn't going to be some easy task. If you make a wrong move, the world could be destroyed. Do you understand?" Lindsey nodded her head seriously.

"I understand. Please tell me what I need to do, and I promise that I will help the sisterhood out the best that I can." Lindsey felt a new sense of strength growing in her. She was scared, and everything had happened to her incredibly fast, but since these people were relying on her, she needed to do everything in her power to not let them down.

It'll take Lindsey some time to understand that she's a witch now, and she'd need to keep this information to herself by any means necessary. Lindsey saw Laurie watching her closely, and Lindsey put on the bravest smile that she could muster. Lindsey knew from this day forward her life would be different, and her task will be difficult, but she knew with her new sisters, she'd make the best of her journey.

Part Two: Attack Against the Sisterhood

Lindsey breathed heavily as she tried her hardest to dodge Laurie's electric storm spells. It had been a full week since Lindsey became a witch and joined the sisterhood in an attempt to defeat Chaos, but she was starting to regret it.

"Can... can we take a quick break?" Lindsey didn't think her lungs could take any more of the harsh breathing. "Ah!" Lindsey cried out and dodged the bolt of electricity that shot straight at her.

"Humph!" Laurie folded her arms and glared at the witch who was supposedly going to be the one who saved all of mankind and the world from Chaos' evil intentions. "I should have known you'd try to give up as soon as the going got too rough," Laurie said and threw her long hair over her shoulder. It was no secret that Laurie was not a fan of her classmate.

"I'm not trying to give up!" Lindsey said, blushing. She honestly didn't understand why Laurie expected her to get the hang of something so quickly. Lindsey knew that she had to become stronger so that she could help the sisterhood out in any way that she could. But she wouldn't be able to do anything if she passed out from exhaustion.

"Oh? Well, it looks like you're throwing in the towel." Every day after school, Lindsey and Laurie trained together. Laurie still looked at Lindsey like she didn't want the twelve-year-old to be there, but she complied with the other sisters' wishes and prepared Lindsey for the upcoming battle.

"I need a quick break! I'm not trying to give up. How do you expect me to do this right if you don't allow me to catch my breath?"

"There are no breaks in a battle. If you go up against Chaos or Serenity, do you honestly believe they will let you take a break?" Lindsey blushed. She understood where Laurie was coming from; however, this wasn't a real battle so she should be able to catch her breath for a few moments.

"No, they wouldn't give me a break, but you can," Lindsey muttered. Just when Laurie was about to say something, Cir walked out of a cloud of purple smoke.

"Sister, please do not be so hard on our Savior. She is new and deserves a quick rest. Remember, you weren't as strong as you are now when you first joined the sisterhood." Lindsey jumped in shock once Cir materialized in front of her. After seeing it as many times as she had, Lindsey was still not used to Cir's technique.

"If we don't speed this process up Chaos will destroy the world," Laurie said exasperatedly. Cir's calm face hadn't looked the least bit disturbed at Laurie's outburst.

"If you try to cram everything you know into her head, she won't remember any of it and would probably be conquered by Chaos," Cir said, and Lindsey shivered in fear. She did not like the sound of that. Laurie stared at Cir for a long while and then she glanced over at Lindsey in irritation.

"Fine, you have ten minutes," Laurie said and mumbled something under her breath before she disappeared. Cir looked at the spot where Laurie had just vanished from for a few moments before she focused her eyes on Lindsey.

"I'm so sorry for our sister's behavior. She can be a little..." Cir searched for the correct words for a few moments. "Intense at times," Lindsey smiled at Cir. Out of everyone at the sisterhood, Cir made Lindsey feel the most comfortable. Except for Laurie, all of the women there were nice, but Cir's mysterious air about her drew

Lindsey to the young girl instantly.

"It's alright. This past week is the most that I've ever spoken to people, especially Laurie. She might seem a little agitated with me at times, but I'm glad that we're getting the chance to talk to each other." Cir nodded her head and waved her hands in front of them. When Lindsey looked to where Cir had waved her hand, she noticed two chairs in front of them.

"You are amazing, Cir." Lindsey's eyes widened in surprise, and Cir gave a soft smile, a rare expression for the light-haired girl.

"Oh, that's nothing," Cir said modestly. "Once you get the hang of things, you'll be able to do these things as well, Savior." Lindsey frowned at the word savior.

"Cir, please call me Lindsey. I appreciate you believe me to be your savior, but it sounds odd." Lindsey thought that if Cir would call Lindsey by her name, then they would be considered friends. Cir thought about what Lindsey had said for a few moments, and Lindsey wondered if the other girl had friends of her own. "Don't you call your friends by their names?" Lindsey asked.

"Friends," Cir repeated and looked at Lindsey confused.

"Yes, your friends. Don't you hang out with your friends on the weekend?" Lindsey asked Cir, and Cir shook her head.

"I spend most of my time researching ways to make the portal stronger and the rest of my time offering support for the sisterhood." Lindsey couldn't believe that this gentle young girl never spent any time with others or had any fun.

"You're just like me," Lindsey whispered, and a small smile spread across her lips. Lindsey was tired of being friendless and spending the majority of her time in the confinements of her bedroom. Lindsey did not want another person to experience the same thing that she's experiencing. "I'm your friend, Cir."

"You're my friend?" Cir asked almost like the words were foreign on her tongue. Lindsey nodded her head enthusiastically.

"Yes, it's not good to always be alone. You deserve to have friends who you can speak with and tell secrets to. You and I both need to get out more and enjoy our childhood. Trying to figure out ways to defeat Chaos shouldn't be the only thing on a preteen's mind." Lindsey took Cir's hand in hers and blushed. "Will you be my friend, Cir?"

Cir couldn't believe how forward the girl was considering that Laurie told her countless of times that Lindsey kept to herself in class. Cir hadn't had anyone she could call a 'friend,' but she did find Lindsey interesting and not just because she's the destined one. The young witch's aura felt the same as hers. It didn't take Cir too long to answer.

"Yes, I'll be your friend!"

*****

By the time that Laurie and Lindsey were done training, Lindsey was dripping with sweat.

"Alright, that'll be all for today. I have homework to do." Laurie said and flipped her hair over her shoulder. Lindsey looked at the other girl and was impressed that she didn't even appear to be remotely winded.

"How... how did I do?" Lindsey asked hesitantly. During the remainder of her training, Lindsey tried her best to do everything that Laurie wanted without giving her too much lip. Laurie glared at Lindsey and then appeared to be thinking. After a few more moments, Laurie's harsh glare softened a little.

"I guess you didn't do a horrible job," Laurie reluctantly said. She didn't want to admit it, but once Laurie gave Lindsey her break, and they resumed their training, Lindsey's speed increased, and Lindsey dodged Laurie's electricity with ease. "I guess you and Cir were right," Laurie mumbled. A broad smile spread across Lindsey's face at Laurie's compliment.

"Thank you. I'm sure that I will become a great witch with your help." Lindsey's heart was pounding in her chest. She was happy that she was starting to get the hang of it, but Lindsey was even more joyous that she had gotten praised by Laurie.

"Cir," Laurie called out, and Cir appeared from a cloud of purple smoke.

"You've done well... Lindsey." Cir said and gave Lindsey a small smile. Lindsey beamed and thanked Cir.

"I don't know how to send myself to my house and her to her house without going with her. Can you do that for us?" Cir nodded her head.

"I'll teach you one day," Cir said. Nodding at the two young girls, they disappeared. One moment Lindsey was looking at Cir and Laurie, the next second she was staring at the wall of her room.

"Wow," Lindsey said amazed.

7

Thank god the day is over with, Lindsey thought as she started putting her books into her book bag. It was Friday and Lindsey was happy for the three-day weekend that they were about to have. The school was having some work done, and it wouldn't be finished until late Monday afternoon. The students were happy they wouldn't have to listen to all of the construction-related noises.

"I have so many things I have to do this weekend that I don't think I'll have enough time in my schedule to hang out." Lindsey looked up towards the sound of the familiar voice. Apparently, Laurie's friends asked her to spend time with them this weekend, and Laurie casually turned them down.

Lindsey knew why Laurie was going to be so busy over the weekend. Laurie told her upfront that they were going to train over the weekend, and Lindsey was excited and a little scared about the arrangement. It'll be nice if she told them that she'd be hanging out with me; technically this wasn't a lie because Laurie was going to be with Lindsey most of the weekend. Unfortunately, it was work related and not friend related.

"That's a shame; maybe we can do something next weekend?" One of Laurie's friends asked hopefully. Laurie flashed her bright smile.

"Of course, if nothing else comes up." Laurie packed her things and left out of the classroom. Laurie told Lindsey that she didn't want to be seen walking with each other, so they planned to meet up at the park. This saddened Lindsey, but she just nodded her head and told Laurie that meeting at the park would be okay. After several moments had passed, Lindsey made her way out of the classroom.

Lindsey made sure she put enough distance between her and Laurie as she trailed behind her. When a few students stopped Laurie to have a quick conversation with her, Lindsey circled them and made her way towards the park.

"You've been walking home every day for the past week! Is everything alright?" Lindsey could hear one of the students ask Laurie.

"Yeah, I'm just trying to get a little more active. The dance team is having tryouts soon, and I want to be in tip-top shape." Laurie said.

"Oh, you look great! You will get on the team with no problem!" Lindsey sighed as soon as she was out of hearing range of the students.

"It must be nice to be complimented," Lindsey said to herself. Most of the time she heard her classmates call her weird or awkward, it was seldom that Lindsey received a compliment. Lindsey remembered that Laurie had praised her the other day and that brought a smile to her face. Laurie hadn't looked like she wanted to give Lindsey that compliment, but she did nonetheless.

Lindsey walked for a few more minutes, and before too long she was at the park. Lindsey walked to a nearby bench and sat down. Looking around the small park, Lindsey noticed that there was nobody there.

"This is where this all began for me," Lindsey said as she recalled the events that had happened over a week ago. Lindsey remembered being so upset that Laurie hadn't come to school that day, so she took a stroll in the park to clear her head. At the park, Lindsey's whole world had changed. She had witnessed the fight between Laurie and an evil witch by the name of Serenity. Things weren't looking good for Laurie, so Lindsey had attacked Serenity with all her might.

"I still can't believe that happened," Lindsey mumbled. Unfortunately, Lindsey was no match for the witch and was thrown out of the way with ease. It appeared that Serenity was going to take her finishing blow, but she ended up aiming it at Laurie at the last moment. That was when Lindsey jumped up because she didn't want either of the girls to get hurt. She got hit, but instead of getting hurt, she became a witch.

"What are you mumbling about?" Lindsey jumped in fright when the sound of Laurie's voice resonated in her ears. Jumping up quickly, Lindsey blushed.

"Don't... don't sneak up on me like that! You almost

gave me a heart attack!" Lindsey yelled while clutching her chest to add more emphasis on how afraid she had been. Laurie rolled her eyes at this.

"You knew I was walking behind you, so why are you surprised?" Lindsey's already rosy cheeks deepened in color.

"You didn't make a sound when you walked up," Lindsey said and shook her head to calm her nerves. "Well, are you ready to go?" Lindsey asked, and Laurie nodded her head.

"Yeah, Cir's going to help train you today as well." Lindsey's face broke into a grin after hearing Cir's name. She knew the young girl didn't go into a battle, but the magic that she could do was phenomenal. Laurie walked closer to Lindsey and gripped her arm.

"With quickness take us to the land
Of the witches where we can try our hand
At getting ready to battle those who wish to bring destruction
Guide us through the wind, give us your protection!"

Lindsey's head started spinning when a strong wind followed by complete darkness took control of her. Sometimes, Lindsey saw different colors when Laurie's spell transported them to the place that was not the earth, Heaven, nor reality. This time, however, Lindsey saw absolutely nothing. She wasn't used to such darkness, so she couldn't help herself when a twinge of fear took over her.

"Don't worry," Lindsey heard Laurie's voice, but her voice almost sounded like a dream. "This was scary for me when I first became a witch too. My power isn't as powerful as Cir's so I can't get us there any quicker. Please put up with the darkness for a while longer." Taking a deep breath, Lindsey stopped herself from shaking, and a few seconds later, they were at the sisterhood's headquarters.

"Where is everyone at?" Lindsey asked, surprised that nobody was in the main hall where they had materialized. Laurie closed her eyes and appeared to have been deep in thought.

"Something doesn't feel right," Laurie said, and instead of the glare she wore when Lindsey was around, Laurie looked disturbed by something. After thinking for a few more moments, Laurie grabbed Lindsey's arm. "We have to find Cir! Something doesn't feel right." If something was indeed wrong, Lindsey wanted to make sure everyone was alright as soon as possible.

"Right, lead the way!" Laurie ran down the long and narrow hallway with Lindsey's arm still clutched in her grip. Laurie's grip was a little painful; however, she endured it. After a short while of running, they came to the massive white room that Laurie trained Lindsey in. Finally letting go of Lindsey's arm, Laurie pushed the door opened and gasped when she saw Cir lying on the ground.

8

Lindsey's heart stopped when she saw her new friend on the floor and Laurie, and Lindsey dashed over to the fallen white-haired girl.

"Cir!" Lindsey shouted as she knelt on the ground next to the girl. Lindsey looked up at Laurie, and she saw how distressed she looked. "Cir!" Lindsey called out again, and this time, Cir's eyes began fluttering open.

"Lindsey... Laurie," Came Cir's quiet voice. Laurie stooped down and pushed her hand towards Cir.

"Grab my hand. It's alright; we're here now." Lindsey stood up and helped Laurie pull Cir onto her feet. The young witch didn't appear to have been hurt. "What happened?" Laurie asked once Cir had regained some of her composure.

"Serenity has figured out a way to travel in and out of the portal," Cir said feebly. "Some of our sisters were guarding the entrance, and out of nowhere, Serenity came out. They tried to detain her, but they were no match. I sensed a commotion, and I went to the Hall of no escape, and I saw our sisters fighting her." Cir paused.

"Are you hurt, Cir?" Lindsey asked, and Cir shook her head. "No... no, I'm fine, Lindsey." Clearing her throat, Cir continued the story. "When Serenity saw me, she threw a fireball at me and unfortunately, I didn't dodge it quickly enough. She ran, and the other sisters followed. I must have fainted from the shock." Cir said and for the first time since she'd known the witch; Lindsey saw Cir blush in shame.

"There's no time to think of a plan. I must follow our sisters and stop Serenity!" Laurie ran over to the middle of the floor.

"Wait, you're going by yourself?" Lindsey asked in surprise. Laurie's electric shock spell was powerful, but Lindsey didn't think it was that powerful. "That's dangerous!" Lindsey said and ran towards Laurie and grabbed her arm.

"Let me go! I must help them!" Laurie said, but Lindsey refused to let Laurie go.

"She's right sister," Cir chimed in and walked over to Lindsey and Laurie. "You are no match for Serenity and at this time; none of us are." Lindsey and Laurie turned to face Cir then. "Serenity created a portal and ran through it. Luckily, our sisters were able to jump in before it closed up. I can re-summon the portal and stop time for a brief amount of time. If they are in the midst of a battle, then their actions would be slower."

"I think that's a good idea," Lindsey said, letting go of Laurie's arm. She might have been the newest witch and member of the sisterhood, but she had years of watching and reading books on witches to understand where Cir was going with this. "I don't think we should go through the portal and fight though if you don't believe that we're strong enough. Can you freeze people in place?"

"I cannot 'freeze' people, but I can stop their functions and cause them not to be able to move for a little while." Laurie placed her hands on her hips then.

"Cir, let's go through the portal and save our sisters. Can you stop Serenity's time long enough to aid us in getting our sisters out?" Cir nodded her head at this. "I don't want Serenity to see you, Cir. I need you to use your shapeshifting abilities." Lindsey's turned quickly so that she could look at Laurie's face to see if she was joking.

"You can shapeshift too?" Lindsey asked in surprise. Cir was even more amazing than she initially believed her to be. Cir gave Lindsey a quick nod and poof! A cloud of purple smoke engulfed Cir's small frame and when it disappeared, in Cir's spot was a little white kitten. "Cool!" Lindsey shouted with glee and jumped up and down excitedly.

"That's enough! This is no time to be worked up over a witch knowing how to shapeshift." Lindsey stopped jumping then and blushed. Laurie was right; they need to hurry up and save their friends. "Re-summon Serenity's portal!" Laurie shouted, and Cir nodded her head.

"Right, stand back." Seeing the little kitten speak was too adorable to Lindsey that she almost started hopping up and down again. "We only have one try, so we must make this one count."

"I know. Also, try not to be seen. I know that you're a cat and the odds of Serenity knowing that you can shapeshift unlikely, I still don't want to take that chance."

"I know. While we're in the portal, I'll try to keep my distance." Cir said, and a round symbol appeared on the floor underneath Lindsey and Laurie. Laurie looked at the portal that Cir just made and then she looked at Lindsey.

"Don't do anything stupid. I don't want you messing up Cir's concentration." Lindsey could tell that Laurie did not want her to go with them, but it wasn't as if they could leave Lindsey at the headquarters by herself. She wouldn't be able to protect their base if some more enemies come out of the portal.

"She'll do fine sister. Believe in her." Cir said and made her way towards the portal.

"You're supposed to call your friends by the names, Cir," Lindsey said as she looked down at the feline.

"Yes, we'll be alright, Laurie because we have Lindsey."

*****

"What is this place?" Lindsey asked once they materialized outside of the portal. It was dark, it smelled like old cheese, and the ground beneath their feet was squishy.

"Hmmm… this is the land of pure evil. Why would Serenity come to this place? Not a female-friendly environment." Cir said as she shook out her white fur. She's never been to the land of pure evil before, but she knew only bad things happened here.

"Let's find them quickly; I don't like it here." Lindsey wasn't surprised by the disgusted look on Laurie's face. The popular twelve going on the thirteen-year-old girl was evidently only used to the finer things in life.

"Yes, it is a bit difficult to walk around on all fours," Cir said, and Lindsey beamed.

"Want me to hold you?" Lindsey happily volunteered. She wasn't allowed to have a cat because her mother didn't like them and all of the stray cats ran away when Lindsey got too close to them.

"No," Laurie said before giving Cir a chance to respond. "We need her behind us. I don't want Serenity to see her." Lindsey muttered, but she didn't say anything else regarding the matter. They had walked for several long minutes before they heard a loud commotion.

"There they are!" Lindsey said, and Cir and Laurie's eyes followed Lindsey's eyes. They saw Serenity blowing fire on her fingers and the women of the sisterhood making a water shield. Something's off, Lindsey thought to herself before she realized what it was. Everyone was moving slow!

"Now's your chance!" Cir said hiding in a shrubbery nearby. "I will stop Serenity's movements and restart our sisters' movements."

"Right," Laurie said and turned towards Lindsey. "Help me guide our sisters, Lindsey. Their movements have been slowed for too long; they will need help getting away." Lindsey could feel a twinge of fear making its way from the pit of her stomach to her throat, but she swallowed it back down.

"Leave it to me." Lindsey was thankful that the slow effects of Cir's spell did not affect them as they made their way towards the battle.

"Humph… I knew if I kept up this charade long enough you two would eventually appear." Serenity said as she moved her head slowly in the direction of Laurie and Lindsey. Serenity smiled momentarily before she jumped up quickly in the air and landed behind Laurie and Lindsey. "Did you honestly think your little 'slow' spell would slow me down?" Laurie and Lindsey gasped once they realized the spell hadn't worked.

9

"I knew something was up when all of your 'sisters' started moving slowly." Serenity said, and Lindsey and Laurie moved forward and turned to face Serenity. She was wearing her signature red, and her eyes were a haunting crimson color. "I didn't think a weakling witch like you could pull off a spell like this, though." Serenity said, eyeing Laurie.

"Tsk! Why are you not effected by the spell?" Laurie asked irritated. She knew that getting her comrades out of this world would be difficult, but she at the very least thought that Cir's spell would work.

"Were you listening to me at all? I told you that your spell was too weak to hold me. I was trained by the Chaos. I think I'm powerful enough to withstand any spell that your group may come up with." Lindsey listened to the transaction between the two girls, and she quickly looked back at Cir. The feline was looking at them from behind the shrubbery.

If the slow spell weren't enough to hold Serenity back, then maybe a complete stop spell would Lindsey thought to herself. Lindsey didn't have enough experience with spells as of yet, so she knew that she wouldn't be able to pull off a spell like that. She also knew that Cir had to keep her presence hidden from Serenity. What should they do?

"I see you brought the destined one," Serenity said eyeing Lindsey. The girl's piercing eyes were enough to make Lindsey shiver in fear. They had to get out of there as soon as possible. Without thinking twice about it, Lindsey shouted which caused Laurie and Serenity to jump in surprise.

"Stop completely spell!" Laurie and Serenity looked at Lindsey in confusion, but Cir knew exactly what Lindsey had wanted. Without hesitation, Cir released her slow spell from that world, and the sisterhood's speed went back to normal.

"What... what happened?" One of the women said in confusion. She remembered that the sisterhood had jumped through the portal to try and capture the evil witch, but she couldn't remember anything after that. The sisterhood's bodies were wobbly and felt like pudding.

"Stop!" Cir whispered and pointed her cat nose in Serenity's direction. Serenity wasn't sure what was going on, but before she knew it, her body's ability to move ceased to exist. She couldn't move!

"What?" Laurie said in confusion and looked at Lindsey.

"There's no time to explain. We need to get our sisters!" Laurie nodded her head and ran over to the witches of the sisterhood.

"We need to go! Now!" Laurie grabbed two of the

women by the arms and started running towards the direction of the portal. Lindsey was about to help the remaining women, but they snapped out of their stupor quickly. Running passed Lindsey, Lindsey looked at Serenity one more time and turned on her heels and started running away.

"I got you Cir," Lindsey whispered and quickly bent down to pick up the white cat in her arms.

"We must hurry. I can't keep the portal open and stop Serenity's movements at the same time in this form." Nodding her head, Lindsey picked up the speed. Soon Lindsey, Laurie, and Cir were back at the sisterhood's headquarters with all of the witches accounted for.

*****

"I see. I hate to admit it, but that was smart thinking on your part, Lindsey." Laurie said tossing her long hair over her shoulder. Lindsey told Laurie and the other witches that she knew that Cir would understand what she wanted if she had shouted "stop." Lindsey informed the women of the sisterhood that to keep Cir's presence hidden from Serenity; she thought that if she called out that and Serenity stopped, then Serenity would believe that Lindsey did the spell.

"Thanks. I didn't have too much time to think about it. I'm glad it worked." Lindsey said smiling at Laurie. Laurie gave Lindsey a small smile back, and Lindsey's eyes widened in surprise. Laurie never looked at Lindsey so kind before, and the girl never smiled at the girl before. It was something so small, but Lindsey was glad to see that Laurie had started warming up to Lindsey.

After realizing what she had done, Laurie sighed and looked away from Lindsey. "Cir, how long can you keep that up?" Cir had regained her body, and Lindsey was a little saddened by that. She liked Cir as a cat. Cir took in a deep breath and turned towards Laurie.

"I can keep it up for a day. Sisters!" Cir called out, and the witches of the sisterhood walked over to them.

"Yes, sister?" They said in unison.

"We need to teach the destined... I mean... Lindsey, some spells. It seems like she's good at coming up with a strategy on the spot, but strategy only goes so far." The women nodded their heads in agreement.

"We haven't held classes since this whole thing began, it'll be good to have a magic class for everyone. Everyone could chip in and help with Lindsey's training while improving themselves." Laurie suggested, and Cir nodded her head.

"That's a splendid idea. I believe if I make this spell strong enough, I'll be able to stop Serenity for a few hours before I'd have to return to this spot. I'll join the class shortly." Cir said and turned her attention back to the task at hand. Nodding her head, Laurie looked at everyone.

"Let's go." Lindsey followed the group of women, and even though they weren't in the best of situations at that moment, she felt happy and right at home. When they rounded the corner of the long narrow hallway, a door opened, and Lindsey saw a classroom that rivaled all others. It was so much more than a typical class. If Hogwarts' students could see this class, they'd be jealous.

"What?" Laurie asked Lindsey when she noticed the girl staring wide-eyed at the classroom.

"Oh, I just thought that the students' of Hogwarts would be jealous if they saw this class." Usually, Lindsey would have said something snippy to Lindsey for comparing the sisterhood's classroom for witches with a fictional class from a fictional story. However, Laurie simply looked around the classroom with its floating chairs and little mists of magic particles floating in the air.

"Yeah, I think they'd envy us." Lindsey's head turned quickly to look at Laurie in shock. The other girl avoided Lindsey's watchful eyes and made her way to a seat. Laurie waved her hand at the floating chair, and it started to descend to the ground. Laurie wouldn't admit this, but the longer she spent time with Lindsey, the more she began to like the girl. I guess you can't judge a book by its cover, Laurie thought to herself.

"How do I get my seat down?" Lindsey asked when she

walked to the desk floating across from Laurie. Lindsey looked at her classmate and blushed. She felt odd that she'd be able to sit next to the popular girl and Lindsey felt giddy as well.

"Think about what you want Lindsey. You want the desk to lower itself so that you can sit down. Will it to lower and it will if you want it bad enough," That sounded easier said than done, but Lindsey closed her eyes and did what Laurie told her to do. Lindsey wished the desk to listen to her, and she mirrored Laurie's motion and waved her hand at the desk.

"Come to me," Lindsey mumbled and opened her eyes. When her eyes opened, Lindsey noticed that the desk lowered itself down slowly in front of her. When the desk was comfortably on the ground, Lindsey grinned and looked at Laurie. Laurie nodded her head and then spoke up.

"Alright, which master is going to go first?" Laurie asked, and whispers resounded through the massive room. Lindsey didn't know what Laurie meant by 'masters,' but she knew this was going to be one of the most exciting classes that she'd ever taken.

10

"Ah!" Lindsey said as the witch by the name of Nina stood up in the front of the class and bent metal with the force of her powers. The class had to explain that the witches of the sisterhood were all masters of a particular type of magic. This was an interesting concept to Lindsey, instead of having head wizards and witches teach a class, it was shown by the students!

"Now, everyone else tries," Nina said, and the students' stood up from their chairs. Lindsey watched as the other students produced a metal object out of thin air, and then used the force taught by Nina to bend the object.

"I've never done any magic before today. Can you help me?" Lindsey whispered to Laurie. The main thing Lindsey and Laurie had been working on was dodging. Lindsey had yet to try to perform any spells.

"Yeah," Laurie walked over closer to Lindsey's desk. "This might be a little hard since we haven't worked on basic magic yet. Just like lowering your desk, you need to think about bending the object in front of you. Here, I created too many magic pipes." Laurie gave Lindsey a small metal pipe, and Lindsey thanked the girl.

"Do I have to chant a spell?" Lindsey asked, and Laurie shook her head.

"No, that's only for more difficult spells. A few words

would be alright for this exercise. Watch me." Laurie grabbed another metal pipe and placed it on Lindsey's desk so that she could see the demonstration better. "If you think about doing something and your will is strong enough, you will succeed!" Laurie took in a deep breath and focused on the metal pipe. "Bend at the force of my power!" Laurie shouted, and the metal pipe bent into a perfect knot.

"Awesome!" Lindsey said and clapped her hands. Laurie looked over at Lindsey and gave her the second smile of the day. The longer they spent time together, Laurie realized that Lindsey was a sweet girl and once she overcame her shyness, she was a pretty cool person to be around. She wouldn't tell Lindsey that, though.

"Alright, give it a try Lindsey," Lindsey grinned and turned towards the metal pipe. She got serious at that moment, and she placed her hand above the object. She focused long and hard, and she willed herself to be powerful enough to bend the metal pipe.

"Bend!" Lindsey shouted. A few seconds passed them by, and Lindsey thought she needed to try again, but the pipe started making creaking noises. It didn't happen as quickly as Laurie's did when she made her pipe bend, but after several long seconds, Lindsey's pipe bent itself. It wasn't a knot, and it wasn't bent to unique angles, but it was bent nonetheless.

"Good job. With practice, you'll get better. Though I think that was a great effort on your first try." Laurie said, and she looked up as Nina approached them.

"Good job sister, you've got a natural talent." Lindsey blushed and looked away modestly.

"I was able to do this because of you and Laurie." Nina smiled and walked around the room and evaluated everyone's work.

"Everyone was able to do it. A lot of you did it better than the last time you did it. Good job." Nina took her seat, and one by one, the masters of a particular magic spell took to the front of the room. Lindsey just knew that she'd struggle a lot, but surprisingly enough, she was able to do all of what she tried, thanks to the help of Laurie.

"I am sorry for the wait. I wanted to make sure the stop spell was strong enough to contain Serenity." Everyone turned towards the door when they heard the sound of Cir's voice.
She looks so exhausted, Lindsey thought as she looked at the young girl. Lindsey could tell that even though Cir wasn't a fighter, which she was easily one of the stronger witches there. "How is our new sister, Lindsey doing?"

"She's doing well." Laurie chimed in and ran her hands through her long hair. "She was able to do all of the spells well." Cir smiled at Lindsey and made her way to the front of the room.

"That is great. As you know, I provide backup to the sisters' here. I will show you how to do an illusion by creating environments that are not there. These are one of the many things that I've mastered." Cir said, and then the classroom's eyes were on her. Cir's eyes turned silver, and then they were no longer at the sisterhood's headquarters. The students were now in a beautiful tropical forest.

"How does she do this?" Lindsey whispered to Laurie. "How was she able to learn this?" Lindsey couldn't believe her eyes when their environment changed. One minute they were in a tropical forest, the next they were in a hot desert.

"Cir is a prodigy. She was born a witch, and she always knew she was a witch. Her mother was a witch, and her father was a wizard. They used to practice in front of her and she pretty much learned from watching. She comes to these classes often to learn other things that she hasn't mastered." Lindsey knew that Cir was amazing, she just hadn't known that the girl was this amazing.

"That's amazing. Where are her parents now?" Lindsey asked. From the few transactions that she had with her new friend, she barely spoke about herself, or her family. Laurie shook her head slowly.

"Three years ago, when Chaos first broke out of the portal that we sealed him in, Cir's parents had a battle with him and his minions. They managed to seal Chaos into the portal again, but Chaos shot a powerful magic spell at them, and we never saw them again." Lindsey gasped in horror. "It's possible that Chaos sent them to a different dimension, but no matter how hard we have tried to locate them, we could never find them."

Lindsey's sad eyes looked at Cir again as she finished her illusion spell. Lindsey couldn't imagine the pain that Cir must be feeling. To lose one's parents and not know anything about their disappearance had to be tough. Lindsey didn't know where Cir's parents were and what she could do to help them, but Lindsey did know one thing. "I'll save them."

*****

"I need to get home now. I have a lot of homework that I need to get done." Lindsey said after everyone finished going through the spell that they'd mastered. Laurie furrowed her brow and folded her arms in contemplation.

"It's time for Lindsey to go now. The portal and the stop spell should hold. The sisterhood cannot interfere with her life, or yours, sister." Cir said walking up behind them. Laurie nodded her head and turned towards Lindsey again.

"Right. Cir, you'll contact us if something happens, right?" Laurie asked, and Cir nodded her head in agreement.

"Of course," Cir said, and Lindsey pushed out the breath

that she'd been holding in. She was sure that Laurie wasn't going to agree to let her leave for the day. Lindsey was as worried about Serenity as the witches of the sisterhood were. But Lindsey knew with Cir's strength and determination, Cir could manage to hold Serenity back as long as possible.

"Cir," Lindsey said and walked over to Cir and embraced her. Cir was taken aback at Lindsey's affection, but she also welcomed it. "Thank you so much for everything." Lindsey pulled back and looked Cir in the eyes. "I promise you that I'll help you out as best as I can." Cir nodded her head. Cir knew that Lindsey was the destined one to defeat Chaos, but there was one thing that Lindsey was sure that the other girl didn't know. Lindsey made a vow to rescue Cir's parents by any means necessary.

"Cir, I hate to ask you this since you're straining real hard by keeping the portal closed and keeping Serenity from moving," Laurie said and ran her manicured hand through her hair. "Can you transport Lindsey and me to our homes?" Cir nodded her head.

"This is no problem for me at all, so please do not feel sorry, sister." Laurie smiled at the younger girl and turned towards Lindsey.

"You did an excellent job today, Lindsey." Lindsey blushed and smiled happily at Laurie's compliment. "I'll see you tomorrow so get some rest." Lindsey nodded her head and said goodbye to everyone within hearing distance of them.

"I look forward to seeing you tomorrow," Cir said, and within a split second, Lindsey couldn't see anything but purple smoke.

11

"Lindsey! Lindsey!" Lindsey wrinkled her eyebrows at the voice. For a dream, this voice sure does sound real, Lindsey thought as she turned over and pulled the sheet up her slender frame. After Lindsey had got home, she spent a lot of time studying and doing homework that wasn't due till Tuesday. Since she spent most of her free time training, she did as much studying as she could when Lindsey wasn't training with Laurie and the sisterhood.

"Lindsey!" The voice said again, and this time, it sounded closer to her ear. "We must return to the sisterhood! Cir and the other ladies need us!" Lindsey opened her eyes and was greeted by darkness. Lindsey looked at her digital clock and saw that it was two in the morning!

"What?" Lindsey asked sleepily still contemplating if this was a dream or not. When she closed her eyes, this time, rough hands pushed her. At this, Lindsey's eyes snapped open again, and she leaned over and turned on her lamp. She nearly screamed when she saw Laurie in her bedroom. "Laurie?!"

"Shush! You're going to wake up your parents." Laurie said, sounding a bit agitated.

"What… How did you get into my bedroom? My house?" Lindsey asked, and her cheeks tinted red. She's never had anybody in her room, and she was almost embarrassed by how childish her room was decorated. Lindsey had pictures of Harry Potter, pictures of the cartoon the Winx Club, and all types of things that her classmates would laugh at her about on her walls.

"Did you forget that I'm a witch? I can get into anywhere that I please. Now get up! We have to get to headquarters."

"It's two in the morning! My parents would freak out if they happen to come in here and I wasn't in my room. I'd be in so much trouble."

"The world would be in so much more trouble if you don't get up!" Laurie raised her voice enough for Lindsey to understand the heat of the situation, but not enough to awaken her family.

"Alright, alright," Lindsey said and raised up out of the comforts of her bed. "Just let me put on some clothes." Lindsey blushed. This was the first time someone has ever seen her in her nightclothes, other than her parents of course.

"Here," Laurie said and waved her hand at Lindsey. Before Lindsey could ask Laurie what she was doing, she found herself wearing the same outfit that she wore several hours ago at the sisterhood headquarters. "We don't have time." Laurie said and grabbed Lindsey's arm.

"Trouble has started, and we must make our way to the fight.

Let us soar through the sky being guided by the moonlight.

Serenity is up to no good, and we must defeat her.

Take us now to the sisterhood headquarters!"

Lindsey was starting to get used to Laurie's chants when they needed to get to the sisterhood's headquarters. She wasn't as afraid this time as darkness surrounded the two witches. They needed to get to the headquarters fast because, by the way, that Laurie was acting, Serenity must have overcome Cir's stop spell.

"Oh no!" Laurie gasped when they finally made it to their headquarters. Lindsey followed Laurie's stares and shrieked when she noticed that the sisterhood's headquarters was in disarray.

"What happened here?" Lindsey asked in horror. All of the sisterhood's equipment had been thrown onto the floor. "Cir!" Lindsey shouted and looked up and down the narrow hallway of their headquarters. "We must find Cir and the others!" Lindsey said quickly.

"Right, stay behind me, Lindsey. We do not know what is amidst here." Laurie said, and Lindsey nodded her head. The girls made two steps and stopped in their tracks when they heard a chilling voice laugh.

"Ha! Did you honestly think you could hold me with that weak spell? I must admit that it caught me off of guard, but I was able to break it as soon as I got over my initial anger." Laurie and Lindsey jumped at the sound of Serenity's voice, and they barely had enough time to dodge the sneak fireball she shot towards them.

"Tsk! Where is Cir, Serenity?" Laurie asked and prepared her electric storm spell.

"Humph, since you foolish witches believe you can keep me trapped in a portal, I merely returned the favor." Serenity said and started walking towards Lindsey and Laurie.

"No!" Lindsey shouted out angrily. Not only did Serenity manage to escape from the portal and break Cir's spell, but she was also able to capture the witches of the sisterhood. "Let them go!" Lindsey raised her voice and got into a defensive stance. She wasn't as experienced in battle as Laurie, but she wasn't going to let Serenity get away with what she'd done.

"Ha! Was Lindsey it? Do you honestly think you could defeat me? You might be the 'destined' one, but you're weak right now." Serenity's red eyes glowed, and her hair blew in a way that looked like she was on fire. "But if I defeat you now, you won't live up to that title!" Serenity shouted those last words and quickly ran towards Lindsey with a fireball forming in her fingers.

"Get out of the way Lindsey!" Laurie screamed. "Electric Storm!" The lightning bolt went flying towards Serenity, and she dodged it with ease.

"You're done!" Serenity shouted, and Lindsey gasped when Serenity was close to her. She had to do something quick. She uses fire magic; maybe I could use the water beam that Aqua taught us earlier, Lindsey thought to herself. During her first class at headquarters earlier that day, or yesterday to be exact, she was taught many things.

"Here goes nothing!" Lindsey said and closed her eyes. "Water Beam!" Lindsey shouted and focused with all of her might. Serenity was about to launch her fireball at Lindsey at close range, but beams of quick water shot her way.

"Ah!" Serenity shouted out in surprise and jumped away from Lindsey's attack. Serenity rubbed her red dress.

"Tsk! When did you learn water moves?" Serenity remembered that one of the witches was able to use water magic earlier, but Serenity dodged it with ease. She wasn't expecting Lindsey to have learned it already.

"That's none of your business, Serenity!" Lindsey said and got into position to attack again. However, just when she was about to call out the spell again, a cloud of purple smoke appeared.

"Cir! Sisters!" Laurie shouted when Cir and the witches of the sisterhood emerged from the smoke.

"Grr…" Serenity growled in anger, and Cir began

walking forward.

"You caught me by surprise before, but that won't happen again. Sisters! Restrain her for interrogation!" Cir said and looked over at Lindsey and Laurie. She was happy to see that her friends were alright.

"Tsk... I must report this to Chaos; you haven't seen the last of me." Serenity said. Just when the sisters were about to close in on her, she was engulfed in flames and was gone.

"She got away!" Laurie snarled.

"This is the last time she'll get away from us. She broke through my defenses when I was going to take a short break and captured us all." Cir said and shook her head in shame. "This is my fault." Lindsey shook her head and walked over and hugged Cir.

"This is not your fault, Cir. You are amazing; we just happened to be dealing with a strong foe." Lindsey let the girl go, and Laurie turned towards her.

"You were amazing, Lindsey. You showed her with that water beam." Lindsey's cheeks reddened at this, but it was not the time to get embarrassed.

"We have to defeat Serenity and Chaos before they destroy the world." At that moment when Lindsey shot the water beam at Serenity, she had felt invincible.

"Yes, we will defeat them, Lindsey, because we have you by our side." The women of the sisterhood surrounded Lindsey at that moment. Serenity might have gotten away today, but this wasn't a defeat for the sisterhood. They will train hard and try their hardest to learn more from Serenity about Chaos' plan. If Lindsey were truly the destined one, then she'd need the help of her friends to bring Chaos and Serenity down.

"No, we'll beat Chaos because we have each other!" Lindsey said. Lindsey looked at the witches in the room and then at Cir and Laurie. These women were her friends and her new family, and she would do her best to stop this evil from taking over the world. Smiling at her new friends, Lindsey thought of the vow she had made. She would save the world from Chaos; she would save Cir's parents from wherever Chaos took them, and she would protect the sisterhood. As the destined one, Lindsey believed she could not fail.

"Sisters, let's get to work!" Lindsey said, and Cir and Laurie grinned.

Part Three: A Chaotic Final Battle

Serenity kneeled on one knee and kept her head down as she listened to the harsh words from her master. She had failed to defeat the sisterhood and had to flee because the witches had overpowered her and caught her. Serenity's red hair shook as her entire body quivered with fear at her master's rage.

"You have failed me on several occasions, Serenity." The evil voice growled. "Do you understand how that makes me feel and look? These second-class witches are making you seem like a novice witch! You are supposed to be the strongest witch ever born! You're meant to be the princess of the new era! This is the era where witches, wizards, and warlocks rule the world and rid this Earth of these pesky humans!" Serenity gritted her teeth and finally looked up at the individual that she could barely see in the darkness.

"My... my master," Serenity began, and her voice quivered. "Please forgive my earlier failures. We miscalculated the sisterhood's skills. The witches by the name of Lindsey, Laurie, and Cir proved to be a little more competent than the rest of them. The 'destined' one, Lindsey, though she is new, she is learning at a rapid rate. A rate that we hadn't previously anticipated," Serenity said, but the mysterious person was hearing none of her excuses.

"Silence!" the voice echoed throughout the chamber. "I do not make miscalculations! You must have given me false information because my plans always work!" the anger seeping through the man's voice gave Serenity the chills. She knew Chaos would punish her, but if Serenity somehow convinced her master to give her another chance, she might avoid the horrible things that her ruler had planned for her.

"My apologies master. I miscalculated the sisterhood's skills which led me to give you a false report." Sighing could be heard throughout the room, and then Serenity heard the sound of a chair squeaking.

"You have disappointed me, Serenity. It would appear that you are not ready to take on the title as the witch princess as of yet," Serenity's head popped up at that moment.

"Master, please just give me a second chance. This time,

I will stop the sisterhood and bring them here to you. You will no longer be trapped in this dreadful place. You will be the king of all magical beings! If you give me another chance, I will show you that I'm meant to wear the crown of a princess." Serenity pleaded with her master to give her another chance, but her master just shook his head.

"Lower your voice when you speak to me!" Serenity jumped, as this startled her and she lowered her head and apologized again. "The sisterhood has been a pain in my side for far too long. They didn't see eye to eye with my vision for our kind. They felt I was too strong and that I didn't keep our kind's best interests in mind. This is why they banished me and sent me to this forsaken place. I will not be made a fool out of because you are not meeting my expectations." The man walked from the darkness and stood directly in front of Serenity.

When he came near her, Serenity shivered and held back her tears. She felt miserable that she had failed her master, and she was miserable that he didn't want to give her another chance. "What are my orders master?" Serenity asked in a small voice.

"You will awaken them," Serenity opened her eyes and stared back into the ghoulishly green and red eyes of her master. His skin was filled with wrinkles and had started to thin with age and from being in such a harsh environment. Purple blotches marred his features, and no amount of magic had helped him. His fingernails were long and sharp, and his teeth matched them.

"Are you sure that you can trust them? They were a part of the sisterhood, and they didn't exactly leave willing." Serenity responded.

"Oh my dear Serenity," the vicious man said with a chuckle in his voice. "Their minds have long since been wiped of their memories. Where their hearts once housed love and compassion, they are now filled with hate and sorrow. When the sisterhood banished me, I took them as compensation. They will work for me, and they will help me destroy the sisterhood once and for all."

"If that is your wish, I will prepare them now." Serenity stood up and bowed to her master. "Be careful master; those individuals are the parents of one of the witches." Serenity said and began walking towards the area where they housed their prisoners. "They might remember her and try to help her out." Serenity wasn't trying to say that her master's plan would fail; she just wanted to make him aware of one of the possible outcomes.

"My plan will work because of how much time and magic I have put into them. They will aid me in my victory against the sisterhood, and I put that on my life as Lord Chaos." A malicious roar of laughter followed Chaos, and though she was being punished, Serenity couldn't help but smile at the future king of the magical beings and the world.

*****

"Lindsey, you've caught on so fast," Laurie said as she watched Lindsey perform the electric storm ability correctly. Once Lindsey had finished, she turned towards Laurie and gave her a broad smile.

"Thanks, it's because I have such a fantastic teacher." Since Lindsey and Laurie had first started working together a few weeks ago, Lindsey's social personality had changed drastically. Lindsey was able to speak to popular girl Laurie without stuttering. Lindsey was able to talk to some of everyone she was around without stumbling over her words.

"What do you think, Cir?" Laurie asked Cir as Cir sat in the corner of the room watching Lindsey and Laurie closely. Cir was able to shapeshift, so to give Lindsey a little more motivation, Cir decided to turn into a cat because cats are Lindsey's favorite animals. Cir stood on all fours and walked over to Lindsey and Laurie.

"Oh you are doing very well, but that's as expected from the destined one, Lindsey." Lindsey gave Cir the biggest smile that she could manage.

"It's because I have you and the sisterhood to thank. I was able to become better in such a short amount of time because of the help that I've received from my new family." Lindsey looked at Laurie and then at Cir, and both of them were smiling at Lindsey. Lindsey and Laurie hadn't initially gotten along because Lindsey was always the odd ball. But since Laurie had gotten to know Lindsey, she had learned that Lindsey was a strong individual who placed the needs of others first.

"No," Laurie shook her head, and Lindsey stared wide-eyed at Laurie. "It's true that we helped you learn the things that you know now. I mean how would you be able to do it if you weren't taught? However, you pushed yourself to excellence." Laurie threw her long flowing hair over her shoulder. "It's taken quite a lot to admit this, but I'm glad you're the destined one. I'm glad that it'll ultimately be you who will stop Chaos from ruining the world."

Lindsey could feel herself becoming sentimental as she listened to the lovely girl who she initially thought would never be her friend. Lindsey had to admit that Laurie wasn't the type of girl that she thought she was. The misunderstanding came about because of Lindsey's and Laurie's opposing school backgrounds. Laurie was one of the most popular girls in the school, and Lindsey was the 'odd' one. There was no wonder why the two seemed like an unlikely pair to become friends.

"Thank you so much, Laurie. You don't know how it makes me feel to hear you say that." Lindsey said dabbing at her eyes. Laurie was officially her first friend at school. Laurie's usually grouchy expression that she had whenever she was around Lindsey was gone. In its place was a sincere smile. Without warning, Laurie walked towards Lindsey and embraced her.

"I'm happy that we'll fight by each other's sides as friends... and sisters. No matter what happens, I know we will be able to stop Chaos' goal to conquer the world." It took Lindsey some time to register that Laurie was hugging her, but when she did, Lindsey reached her hand out towards Cir.

"Come on, Cir," Lindsey said. "You're our friend too, and we need you." Ever since Lindsey had first become a sister, Cir had acquired love that she thought she'd never received again since her parents were gone. The friendships that she had made filled a void that was left in Cir's heart. Still a cat, Cir leaped into Lindsey's outstretched arms, and Lindsey brought Cir in so that they all were hugging. With Laurie, Cir, and the rest of the sisterhood by each other's side, there was no way Chaos would be victorious.

12

"Lindsey?" Lindsey's mother called out to her as soon as she walked through the front door.

"Yes, mom it's me," Lindsey was done with her training for the day, and she needed to get caught up on some homework. Lindsey's mother came out of the kitchen then to greet her.

"You're home later than usual," Lindsey told Laurie and Cir that she didn't have a lot of time that day to practice her magic because she had a lot of homework, so Lindsey said to Cir that she didn't have to use a human duplication spell. "Is everything alright?" Everything technically wasn't alright because there was a crazy wizard who wished to destroy the world, but Lindsey couldn't exactly tell her mother that. Lindsey decided to tell her mother the closest thing to the truth that she could think of.

"Everything's okay mom, I... hung out with some friends today." Lindsey's mother, Amy, raised her eyebrow at this.

"You were hanging out with some.... friends?" Amy asked slowly almost like she didn't believe what her daughter had just told her. To her mother's knowledge Lindsey never hung out with anyone afterschool because every time Lindsey, Laurie, and Cir were training, Cir came up with a fake Lindsey and sent her to Lindsey's home. It was only natural that her mother was surprised that she was hanging out with friends when she was 'technically' always at home. Lindsey had also made a choice not to tell her mother about Cir and Laurie because she didn't want to let anything slip.

"Yes mom, I have friends now," Lindsey grinned at that because that statement was the full truth.

"I see you've finally broken out of your shell. You do seem a lot more chipper than what you normally are. Bring them over to the house sometimes; I'd love to meet them." Amy turned quickly as the teapot on top of the stove started whistling. Lindsey thought about what her mother had just said.

"Other than at the park, has Cir ever been outside of the sisterhood and the different realms?" Laurie had lightened up to Lindsey, so it was a strong possibly that Laurie would accept an invitation to come to Lindsey's house, but what about Cir? Has anyone ever invited the young girl to their homes for a slumber party? Whatever the case may be, Lindsey had it in her mind to ask both Cir and Laurie to spend the night at her house one day.

"It'll have to be once all of this is over, though," In Lindsey's heart, she knew that Serenity wasn't going to attack them again. Lindsey might have been the new witch at the sisterhood, but she had this overwhelming sense that Chaos would make his move next, not Serenity! "I would like to see the man behind the kidnapping of Cir's parents and the monster who wishes to take over the world."

It had been a few weeks since Lindsey learned from Laurie about the battle that happened between the sisterhood and Chaos a few years ago.

Even though the sisterhood was victorious when it came to sealing Chaos away, he took Cir's parents away, the ones who had made sure that he'd never be able to harm anyone with his diabolical ideas. When Lindsey was informed that she was the destined one who would ultimately destroy Chaos, she knew that with the help of her friends she'd be able to live up to their expectations. When Laurie told Lindsey what Chaos did to Cir's parents, she made it her goal to save them as well. "Even though Cir has the sisterhood, she needs her parents as well."

"Lindsey, your lunch is ready!" Amy called out, and Lindsey followed the smell of the food.

"Thanks, mom. I have some work to catch up on so I'll be in my room." Lindsey took her burrito then and made her way to her room. For a brief couple of hours, she put the thoughts of defeating Chaos, the thoughts of being a witch and the thoughts of a sleepover with her two best friends to the back of her mind.

*****

"Lin... Lin..." Lindsey heard a faint voice as she slumbered. The voice belonged to a female, but Lindsey couldn't figure out if she recognized it or not. "Lindsey!" Lindsey jumped up in fright at that moment. Lindsey almost screamed when she saw Laurie sitting on the edge of her bed.

"Laurie?" Lindsey narrowed her eyes and looked around. It was nighttime, but she couldn't remember ever falling asleep. Lindsey guessed that the strain on her body from training with the sisterhood and the strain on her mind from studying had taken its toll on her body. "When did I even fall asleep?" Lindsey asked herself, forgetting that Laurie had woken her up.

"We must leave, Lindsey. I'm worried about the sisterhood." Laurie said as she shook Lindsey softly. Lindsey's eyes widened in surprise at the concerned expression that marred Laurie's lovely features.

"Right," Lindsey said, wasting no time. Lindsey got out of her bed and looked down at her clothes. I don't remember falling asleep, but I did change into my nightclothes, Lindsey thought to herself. "Change," Lindsey whispered and waved her hand down the length of her body. Laurie, Cir, and a few other people had taught Lindsey how to use her magic to change outfits. In a matter of a few short seconds, Lindsey was wearing her favorite black shorts with a pink shirt covered in rhinestones.

"Nice, you're getting better at that," Laurie said and momentarily grinned at Lindsey.

"Do you think we'll be back before the night is over? I don't want my parents to come in, and I'm not here," Laurie shrugged her shoulders.

"Hopefully everything is alright at the headquarters. I haven't heard anything from Cir, and I'm a little worried." Cir gave Laurie an update on the well-being of the headquarters three times a day; morning, afternoon, and night. Cir hadn't given Laurie the night report, which had alarmed Laurie. Lindsey didn't like Laurie's response, but it couldn't be helped.

"Okay, I guess nothing's absolute. I'm ready." Lindsey said, and Laurie nodded her head and grabbed Lindsey's arm.

"This night is cold and filled with Dreary.
The moonless night has left us weary.
Please guide us through the evening's air,
Take us to the sisterhood's lair!"

Lindsey had gotten used to disappearing and going into the dimension where Laurie's powers took them. She no longer shook in fright as the darkness took them over because she knew that it wouldn't last long. She had yet to master this ability, though. The most Lindsey was able to do transport herself from one room in a building to another room in the same building.

"You seem more... relaxed this time." Laurie commented when she noticed that Lindsey wasn't shaking like she normally did when they traveled this way.

"I'm used to it now, besides I cannot always be afraid. I need to be in top condition if I want to protect my friends from something. If I'm always incredibly scared, I'll be more of a nuisance than a help." Laurie was impressed by Lindsey's response. What Lindsey said sounded like something similar to what Laurie might have told her if she thought the girl was scared. Laurie cracked a smile at that, and that was when they yielded to the light.

"Well... it looks normal here," Lindsey commented as they appeared in the main hallway. Nothing seemed destroyed or even out of place.

"No," Laurie said and looked around. "Something's wrong here, something doesn't feel quite right," Laurie commented and looked around. Laurie understood why Lindsey felt that everything was alright because everything looked the same. However, Laurie had learned a long time ago not to assume that just because something looks a certain way that everything was fine. "It feels different here, more sinister."

"Alright, let's look for Cir," As the two of them walked through the corridors, they noticed that the place felt empty. "Where are we going?" Lindsey asked once they had turned down a hallway that Lindsey had never been down before.

"Some of the witches live here. Their bedrooms are

down this hall." A lightbulb blinked in Lindsey's mind when Laurie told her that. Of course, there would be bedrooms for the others without a home or family. The sisterhood's headquarters wasn't their place of business; it was also their home.

"Cir," Laurie called out and knocked on what Lindsey assumed to be Cir's bedroom door. Laurie paused for a moment waiting to see if she could hear the young witch's voice.

"Cir," Lindsey mirrored Laurie's actions, but took it one step further and placed her hand on the doorknob. "Sorry, but we're coming in," Lindsey warned and opened the door. When Lindsey and Laurie entered the bedroom, they were shocked to see Cir sitting on her bed staring directly at them.

"I see that you two have finally arrived," Lindsey and Laurie froze in their spot. That wasn't the sweet sound of Cir's voice. That voice was deep, dark, and malicious; a voice is fitting for the evil mastermind Chaos.

13

As soon as Lindsey and Laurie heard Cir's voice, Laurie got into a fighting stance.

"Wait!" Lindsey shouted and wrapped her arm around Laurie's. "Don't hurt Cir!" Lindsey cried out. She knew that everything looked bad, but as she stared at the person in front of them, Lindsey still saw Cir, even though it wasn't Cir's voice.

"Lindsey, that is not Cir," Laurie pulled her arm from Lindsey, but she kept a steady eye on the young witch. "What have you done to Cir?" Laurie asked angrily, and the deep voice chuckled.

"Why, I didn't do anything to your precious Cir. If anything, she's the one who kept me captive in a world unfit to be lived in.

"We only trapped you in there because you wished to destroy all of humanity! Why would we let someone like you roam the Earth freely? You're a criminal, Chaos!" Laurie spat Chaos' name out of her mouth like his name was sour.

"Humph," Chaos stood up then and looked at Lindsey. "So this is Lindsey the destined one?" It was hard for Lindsey to comprehend hearing the voice of Chaos, but seeing the small stature of her friend, Cir. "I expected you to be something else. All I see is a twelve-year-old girl who barely knows how to tie her shoes." Lindsey was offended by Chaos' unnecessarily cruel words, but there were more pressing issues at hand then.

"Release Cir and show yourself!" Lindsey demanded. How dare Chaos waltz into the sisterhood's headquarters and take control of Cir's body. Chaos frowned at that moment and placed his hands on Cir's hips.

"You can't kick me out of the headquarters when I was in line to become the sisterhood's leader." Lindsey's eyes widened at that and Chaos made Cir smile. "What? Are you surprised that a man was going to run the sisterhood's headquarters? Stranger things have happened my dear, but like I was saying, this was and still is my home."

"The sisterhood will never allow you to come back after what you've tried to pressure us to do. We will not destroy humans just because they don't meet your 'standards' as living beings!" Laurie screamed and prepared her electric storm attack. Chaos snickered at the girl's attempts to try to be intimidating.

"Be about where you're aiming that electricity, girl," Chaos said manically. "You might hear my voice, but this body is borrowed. Hurt me, and you'll hurt Cir." Laurie's eyes widened at that. "I didn't come to fight; I came to offer you two a deal."

"We'll never accept a deal from you!" Lindsey said in anger. She didn't want Laurie to attack Chaos because he was using Cir's body, but that didn't mean they were going to listen to Chaos because of the way that he looked at that moment.

"Lindsey's right, we don't want to hear anything that you have to say. I will find out how to take you from Cir's body without hurting her. Do not underestimate the sisterhood's power!" Chaos was getting rather bored with Laurie and Lindsey and decided they weren't worth his time to be bothered anymore.

"Suit yourself. I was going to offer you two a haven once I take over the world, but you two blew it with your disobedient mouths. I'll leave for today, but know that the next time I come, it'll be the real me." With that said, Cir fell backward and landed down roughly on her bed.

"Cir!" Lindsey and Laurie called out in unison and made their way to Cir. Cir didn't respond at first, but the young witch stirred when they pushed her.

"What... what happened?" Cir asked, and Lindsey was happy that Cir had turned back to normal.

"Cir, you will not believe it," Lindsay said and started telling the girl everything that had happened.

*****

Laurie and Lindsey woke up all of the women stationed there and told everybody what had transpired.

"It looks like Chaos used a deep sleep spell so that you wouldn't awaken if I called out to you for help," Cir said as she looked at her sisters one by one. Lindsey had wondered why the headquarters had been real quiet All of the sisters who were on duty had all one by one felt the urge to sleep. "I can't believe I fell prey to him," Cir said, shaking her head in disbelief. "To have someone take over my body with no recollection."

"Cir, it isn't your fault," Laurie said and looked the young girl in her eyes. "Chaos isn't like Serenity, so naturally he'd be stronger. He caught you off of guard. He caught all of us off guard." Laurie tried her best to help lessen the guilt that Cir was undoubtedly feeling at that moment. The fact that Chaos was able to allow his consciousness to escape the portal had disturbed Laurie.

"I might be out of place to say this," Lindsey began. "But I can't help but think that we're going to have to fight Chaos and soon at that. I don't know too much about him or his history, but if he was able to do that to Cir, I fear he has other tricks up his sleeves." Chaos had been trapped inside of the portal for a very long time, and Lindsey was sure that he had practiced some new magic.

"Lindsey's right. We must practice harder, and we must be ready for everything." Laurie said and looked around the room.

"I don't believe he'll be back tonight. Chaos came to us today because he was warning us. Lindsey... Laurie, I don't want to keep you from your sleep and your homes longer than you need to. Please return home and come back once you are rested."

"But Cir," Lindsey started, but Cir shook her head.

"He won't be back again tonight, Lindsey. Besides, it's late, and your body needs rest. If he did come back, neither of you would be able to perform to the best of your abilities." Lindsey bit her lip to hold back the tears that threatened to spill from her eyes. Lindsey wondered how someone so young could be so mature. Laurie looked at Cir and sighed.

"She's right Lindsey," Laurie said finally. "I do know how you feel. I don't want to leave the sisterhood either. But for tonight, we need to." Laurie looked at all of the witches in the room then. "We didn't see anything damaged or missing, but it would be wise if you did a sweep of the place to make sure." With that said, all of the witches vanished leaving behind Lindsey, Laurie, and Cir.

"Alright," Lindsey said defeated. Cir was right, after all, Lindsey's body felt drained of energy. If there had been a battle that night, they would have more than likely lost. "We'll be back in the morning," Lindsey added, and Cir nodded her head.

"Until then. Have a good night." Lindsey walked over to Cir and hugged her. Cir accepted Lindsey's embrace without hesitating. Once Lindsey let Cir go, Laurie hugged her as well.

"Cir?" Laurie said, and Cir already knew exactly what she wanted.

"Of course," Cir waved her hand in front of Lindsey and Laurie, and after a few seconds, the two of them vanished into a cloud of purple smoke.

14

Lindsey didn't sleep well at all once she got back from the sisterhood. She tossed and turned all night and could not stop thinking about Cir and Chaos. It was apparent that Chaos was more skilled than the red-haired witch. The way that he was able to take over Cir's body sent a shiver up and down Lindsey's spine.

"Am I the destined one to defeat him?" Lindsey asked, sitting up in her bed. She had learned a few spells to protect herself, but could she defeat a wizard with years and years of experience under his belt? "I've only been a witch for a month," Cir was sure that Lindsey would defeat the mighty Chaos, but Lindsey was starting to doubt how accurate Cir's psychic abilities were.

"Lindsey?" Lindsey jumped when a voice called out her name, and a knock ensued on her bedroom door. After the scare that she had undergone last night, it wasn't a surprise that the girl was so jumpy.

"Ah! Come in," Lindsey said and quickly got out of bed. Her mother opened the door then as she placed the mug, filled with coffee without a doubt, to her lips.

"What's wrong? You're acting like you've seen a ghost or something." Her mother asked, concerned and Lindsey shook her head quickly.

"I just woke up when you knocked on my door. I was probably having a nightmare, and the knock scared me,"

The sense of dread that Lindsey was feeling was no nightmare. It was a reality.

"Do you want to talk about it?" her mother asked and walked into the room. Lindsey couldn't talk about anything that was happening around her, and it hurt Lindsey to know that. Her mother wouldn't believe her anyway; she'd think that it was all in her imagination. This was incredibly rough on Lindsey because she always told her mother everything.

"Mom, have you ever had a lot of people expect great things from you, and you end up failing them?" Lindsey was starting to think that she might let the sisterhood down instead of living up to their expectations. Amy wrapped her arms around her daughter then.

"Lindsey, if people have high expectations of you, it's because they know you'll be able to do something. It sounds like to me that you're second-guessing yourself because of this praise. I know that you've been keeping something from me and even though I'd rather that you tell me, I won't push you to do so. Know that as long as you put your mind to something, you'll be able to do it."

Lindsey looked up at her mother when she said the words that Laurie and Cir consistently said to her.

"If I believe in myself, then I'll be able to do it?" Lindsey repeated. As soon as she said that a sense of confidence washed over her once self-doubting self. She would be able to defeat Chaos because she was the destined one. The all-powerful Cir wouldn't have told her otherwise if it was false. Lindsey stood on her tiptoes then and kissed her mother on the cheek.

"Thanks, mom," Lindsey said, and her mother smiled back at her.

"Anytime," Lindsey and the sisterhood might have a limited amount of time to train, but that didn't mean they should throw in the towel and call it quits. When Lindsey has a hard test coming up, she will study for it, and she'd immediately know that she's going to do well on the test. Lindsey could look at the upcoming battle with Chaos the same way. Even though Chaos is strong, she'd study the right material to defeat him.

"I can do this," Lindsey said, looking at the Harry Potter picture on her wall. Looking at that picture always gave Lindsey confidence. In a way, Lindsey thought she was so much like Harry. He was the one who lived, and she was the destined one. Harry was able to defeat his enemies with minimal experience so she was positive that she'd be able to do so as well.

"Breakfast is ready," Amy said and made her way out of Lindsey's room. "Lindsey, whatever obstacle is standing in your way…. just know that you will overcome it," Lindsey grinned a broad grin and followed her mother into the kitchen.

*****

The sisterhood was livelier than ever as the witches sparred with each other.

"Electric Storm!" Laurie shouted and aimed her attack at Lindsey. Lindsey stood her ground and concentrated real hard at the spell coming her way.

"Metal Armor!" Lindsey shouted and held up her hand. Lindsey's spell made a shield in front of her so when Laurie's spell hit it; it caused Lindsey no damage.

"Good job!" Laurie shouted as she tried to catch her breath. It took a lot for Lindsey to catch her breath as well because they were both working hard and moving fast.

"I was wondering," Lindsey paused and Laurie got out of her fighting stance.

"What is it?" Laurie asked and flipped her long hair over her shoulder.

"When do we get our brooms?" Laurie looked at Lindsey for a long while before she did something so very uncharacteristic of her. She laughed! "Hey, what's so funny?" Lindsey asked and blushed. The witches of the sisterhood stopped what they were doing and looked at the two girls curiously. "It's... it's not funny!" Lindsey said blushing.

"I know... I know," Laurie said and wiped a tear out of her eye. "In reality, witches do not use brooms, we teleport." Lindsey's blush deepened at that. After being with the witches for a full month, Lindsey had yet to see any of them ride on a broom. She didn't know why she didn't think that teleportation was the sole means by which they got around.

"That was a dumb question for me to ask," Lindsey said hiding her face. Of course, witches and wizards in real life won't be exactly like the ones on TV. Lindsey waited for Laurie to make fun of her, to humiliate Lindsey more than what she was already feeling, but when it didn't come she was confused.

"It's not your fault Lindsey. You still haven't been here long enough, so we don't expect you to know everything. Many of the sisters hear believed that we'd be flying on brooms and they're older than you. It was funny, but I wasn't laughing at you Lindsey."

Lindsey's eyes widened at the fact that Laurie had just comforted her. The other girl no longer looked down at her; she no longer thought Lindsey was awkward. It wasn't the right time to do this, but Lindsey felt like it was now or never.

"Laurie, when all of this is over, and we defeat Chaos," Lindsey paused, but she urged herself to continue. "Do you want to have a sleepover at my house?" There, I finally said it, the once shy girl thought to herself. Laurie didn't hesitate to give Lindsey her answer.

"Of course, we are best friends after all." Hearing Laurie

say that caused Lindsey to break out into a goofy grin. Not only did Laurie consider Lindsey, her friend, but she viewed the girl as her best friend. "I'm sorry about how I treated you before. You are not some odd and crazy girl. You are a bright and kind witch who will save the world."

"No, we'll save the world. I'll make sure to invite Cir as well. She's our best friend as well." Lindsey couldn't invite everyone at the sisterhood because Lindsey, Laurie, and Cir were the only kids there. Laurie smiled at Lindsey then and hugged her.

"I'm glad that I have gotten to know you. Even though it was because of unfortunate events, I don't regret anything." Lindsey could feel tears of happiness forming in her eyes, but before she could thank Laurie for her kind words, they heard a crash from the other room.

"Ah!" a voice screamed, and there was no doubt in the sisterhood's mind that the voice belonged to Cir.

"Cir!" Laurie and Lindsey called out and made their way towards the direction of Cir's voice. They hustled into the main room, and they saw Cir staring wide-eyed towards a black portal.

"What the?" Lindsey said confused. Standing right at the entrance to the portal was a man and a woman, both whom Lindsey did not recognize. Lindsey turned towards the rest of the sisterhood to ask who these strange people were, but every one of them stood there speechless. Lindsey knew the people there were threats, but Cir's reaction shocked Lindsey the most. The girl who always had a neutral expression looked almost as if she was going to cry. Whoever these people were, it apparently had taken a toll on Cir's emotions.

"Mom... Dad?" Lindsey's mouth fell opened once Cir revealed the identities of the sisterhood's attackers.

15

"Mom... Dad?" those words kept playing over and over again in Lindsey's mind. She couldn't understand what was happening. Lindsey didn't know if Cir's parents had finally managed to come back to the sisterhood after being trapped god knows where in a different dimension, or if they were now enemies of the sisterhood. Lindsey took a step forward towards Cir and the intruders, but Laurie quickly placed her hand on Lindsey's shoulder.

"Stay back! They're... they're dangerous!" Laurie said, and Lindsey turned quickly to look at Laurie. Laurie looked as if she saw ghosts! If they were as dangerous as Laurie seemed to think, they needed to get them away from Cir.

"Cir! Come over here with us!" Lindsey shouted, but Cir appeared not to have heard Lindsey. Instead, Cir started walking closer to them!

"Where... where have you been? Why are you attacking the sisterhood? Why are you attacking me?" Cir said, as she mindlessly walked closer to her parents.

"No Cir! It's a trap!" Laurie screamed, but Cir shook her head.

"These are my parents. This is no trap." Cir said in a voice that barely sounded like her own. Seeing her parents after so long had messed with her mind. Cir asked her parents' many questions, but they didn't answer any of them. Lindsey could feel that something was incredibly off then and just as Cir got even closer to her parents, Lindsey's fear was confirmed. Cir's father lifted up his hand and a dark ball of power formed inside of it.

"No!" Lindsey screamed, and without thinking, Lindsey teleported herself so that she was directly next to Cir. Lindsey took the girl in her arms and jumped back barely dodging the spell.

"Tsk!" her father said, visibly upset that his attack didn't connect.

"Are you okay, Cir?!" Lindsey asked as her heart pounded hard against her chest. She didn't know how she had pulled that one off, but Lindsey was glad that she had. Cir blinked her eyes a few times before resting her lavender ones on Lindsey's.

"Yes... yes, sorry that was a close one." Cir said, and for a moment she almost looked like her normal self.

"A close one indeed. How marvelous would it have been for the young prodigy Cir to be destroyed by her parents?" A dark and sinister voice called out from behind the still opened portal. Lindsey had heard that voice before. That cold, dark, and soulless voice belonged to the one and only...

"Chaos!" Laurie yelled out at the top of her lungs.

"Ha! Ha, ha! Didn't expect to see me so soon, huh?" Chaos said and materialized out of the portal. Lindsey frowned angrily. She'd had a feeling that he'd come back for the sisterhood soon, but she hadn't thought it would have been this soon. "I hope that you don't mind that I brought friends along this time?" Cir shook her head, and Lindsey couldn't believe the expression on Cir's face then. She couldn't remember ever seeing the girl with this expression, but Lindsey was pretty sure that Cir was angry.

"What have you done to my parents?" Cir yelled at Chaos and stood up. Cir didn't go into battle, she offered support, but at that moment, Cir looked as if she was ready to take on a herd of evil witches.

"What have I done to them? I haven't done anything to them. The question that you need to ask is what did the sisterhood do to me that has caused me to help your parents realize how wrong the ways of the sisterhood are." Chaos said and walked over to Cir's parents. He placed his hands on both of their shoulders and grinned. "Like you, I've made great friends who can appreciate my vision of the world."

"That's… that's a lie!" Cir yelled. "My parents were the ones who locked you away! There is no way they would go along with your world domination plan. You've corrupted their minds. You're controlling them the same way that you controlled me!" Cir shook as she spoke, but Lindsey held onto the girl tightly to steady her.

"That's enough, Cir," Laurie said, finally gaining her composure. "This... this is surprising, but blowing up and showing your anger is precisely what Chaos wants. He wants to use this weakness against you so that he can defeat us quickly." Laurie walked in front of Lindsey and Cir and got into her fighting stance. "I don't know what you did to them, but we will get them back, and in the process, we will defeat you!"

"Such a pathetic threat from a pathetic little girl," Chaos said and chuckled, revealing sharp teeth. Hearing Chaos call Laurie pathetic ignited a flame in the popular girl's body. She wasn't going to let Chaos get away with everything he had done. "Hah!" Laurie screamed and ran forward towards Chaos.

"Laurie!" Lindsey yelled out. What is she doing? Doesn't she know how much danger she is putting herself in just by running towards the enemy without a plan? Lindsey looked at all of the other witches and noticed that they were standing in the same spot with their eyes wide open. They were so afraid that he had returned that they didn't know what to do.

"Electric storm!" Laurie called out, and a bolt of electricity came out of her fingers. Laurie thought that Chaos could easily dodge her electric attack if she were far enough away from him. At close range though, no matter how powerful of a wizard he may have been, even he wouldn't be able to dodge her attack.

"Fool," Chaos said and snapped his fingers. Cir's mother jumped directly in front of Chaos and held out her hand.

"Repel," she said, sounding almost like a robot. Laurie's electric storm spell bounced back at Laurie and hit her straight on.

"Ah!" Laurie yelled as she fell backward to the ground.

"Laurie!" Cir called out to her and ran towards her. "Are you okay?" Cir asked Laurie and Laurie placed her hand on her shoulder, where she had been hit.

"Just... a scratch" she managed to blurt out. Cir looked at her mother then.

"Stop! Can't you see that Chaos is controlling you? Snap out of it! Snap out of it!" Cir cried out to her parents.

"Sorry, but your parents can't hear you anymore. They only hear me, their master." Chaos laughed, and Lindsey balled her fists into balls at her sides.

"What are you doing?" Lindsey called out, looking back at the witches of the sisterhood. "We must protect the sisterhood! We must protect the world!" Lindsey called out, and all at once, the witches found their courage.

"This is the moment we've been training for sisters! Attack!" With that said the witches of the sisterhood attacked with all of their powers combined. Fire, water, ice, the wind, earth, all of the elements connected so that they could make one powerful attack.

"Wait! They're still my parents!" Cir cried out, but they didn't listen to her. Anyone who tried to attack the sisterhood was an enemy. With all of their might, they blasted the spell towards Chaos and Cir's parents. "No!" Cir cried out in anguish. She understood why they would attack them. Technically her parents were working for Chaos, but they were still her parents.

"Ha, your powers are useless." Came Cir's father's robotic voice. Without hesitating at all, he stood in front of the huge powerful ball of spells coming their way and held out his hands. "Absorb." He murmured. The combined magic spells that the sisterhood had worked so hard to create was immediately absorbed into his hands.

Lindsey needed an opening! Cir didn't specialize in combat so Lindsey knew the girl wouldn't be able to fight. Plus, Lindsey was pretty sure that the girl wouldn't fight against her parents even though they were being controlled by Chaos.

"Think Lindsey, think!" Lindsey said to herself and watched as her sisters all went to attack Cir's parents with magical spells. "Nothing's working! They're too strong!" Lindsey said to herself as nerves took over her entire being.

"Looks like it's just you and me," Lindsey heard a voice in her ear, and she turned quickly to see the dreadful

Chaos standing right next to her.

16

"A scared little girl like you is supposed to be the destined one? Don't make me laugh," even though as Chaos said that, he let out a hearty laugh anyways.

"I will defeat you!" Lindsey said and jumped backward. Lindsey looked towards Cir and Laurie and noticed that Cir was busy assisting Laurie with her wounds. The rest of the sisterhood was fighting Cir's parents, so that left just Chaos and Lindsey.

"Your chances of beating me are tiny, child," Chaos said smiling. "But let's make a deal. I'll allow you to be a part of my Kingdom. Serenity was originally going to be the princess of the new Kingdom, but I believe you're a more fitting choice!"

"I would never join forces with someone who wants to destroy the world," Lindsey yelled. Lindsey had no choice at that moment, she had assumed that she would receive help from the sisterhood when it came to fighting Chaos, but Chaos' new allies were not a part of the original plan.

She was scared and inexperienced, but if the sisterhood believed she was the destined one, then she would show Chaos how strong she was! "Fireball," Lindsey screamed, and balls of scorching fire flew from her fingertips.

"Humph!" Chaos stepped away from Lindsey's attack. Serenity wasn't the only one who knew how to use fireballs.

"Frostbite," Lindsey yelled, but Chaos dodged that move as well.

"You're a too slow girl. Give up,"

"I'm not too slow, you are!" Lindsey yelled, grinning. Chaos looked down at his leg and noticed some of the ice had, in fact, gotten to him. However, the ice didn't come from the front of his leg; it came from the back.

"Curse you," Chaos said, growing angry. He couldn't believe that Lindsey had landed a sneak attack on him without him knowing. "Meteor," Chaos said, and large meteors began falling from the ceiling.

"Ah!" Lindsey screamed.

"Watch out, Lindsey!" Laurie stood up and started running towards Lindsey; however, Cir's mother jumped in front of her. Apparently, the sisterhood witches were no match for the couple.

"Stop mother," Cir ran over towards her mother, but she was quickly repelled back when she touched her.

"Don't touch her! She has a repel spell surrounding her body!" Laurie said. Cir felt hopeless. She'd watched her parents fight for quite some time by then, but they hadn't displayed any signs of weakness. Meanwhile, Lindsey dodged the meteors left and right. All of the dodging exercises that she had practiced with Laurie were starting to pay off.

"I need to end this quickly!" She could tell that Chaos was an older man by how thin and blotchy his skin was. If she were lucky, he'd just run out of breath. "No, I have to wait for the right chance," Lindsey whispered to herself.

"Stand still! You're like a bug that doesn't know when just to get stepped on." Lindsey could tell the longer she dodged Chaos' attack, the more irritable and less focused he got.

"I got it!" Lindsey screamed and started running quickly towards Chaos. Her loud outburst took Chaos by surprise, but he readied his attack.

"I got you now!" Chaos said, and his arm became engulfed in flames. The sisterhood was as good as destroyed because without the destined one they nor the world stood a chance. Lindsey had predicted a head-on attack from Chaos, so at the last moment, she used all of her might teleport behind Chaos. "What?!" Chaos shouted, confused that Lindsey had disappeared.

"Vine wrap!" Lindsey called, and thick vines emerged from the ground and wrapped themselves all around Chaos' arms, legs, and torso. They were so tightly wrapped around Chaos that he was unable to move.

"How is... how is this possible?" Chaos asked. "You two, attack the girl! Attack the destined one!" Chaos called out.

"Lindsey, the necklace around Chaos' neck! Destroy the necklace around Chaos' neck." Cir shouted just as her parents made a b-line for Lindsey. Lindsey looked at Chaos' thin neck and saw a glowing necklace around it.
"No!" Chaos called out, but it was too late. Lindsey grabbed the necklace from around Chaos' neck and stepped on it until it broke into tiny little pieces. Once the necklace was broken, Cir's parents stopped dead in their tracks.

"It's finally over..." Cir's father said and dropped to his knees. When Lindsey saw Cir's parents stop, she knew that they were back to normal.

*****

"You're cheating! How could you win five games in a row?" Laurie shouted as she flipped her hair over her shoulder.

"Right, you didn't even know how to play this game until I showed you how to do it. Laurie, why are we losing to a cat?" Lindsey sighed. It had been a week since the sisterhood had defeated Chaos and Lindsey had finally gotten her slumber party with her two best friends.

"Oh, don't be a sore loser. And I'm playing as a cat because cats are lucky." Cir said as she flipped over a card using her psychic abilities.

"I thought cats brought bad luck?" Lindsey asked confused, and the silver cat shook its head.

"No, black cats bring bad luck," Cir said and made Lindsey draw four cards again.

"Ugh!" Lindsey sighed and pulled four cards. Despite losing horribly to Cir in Uno, Lindsey and Laurie were having the time of their lives. After the battle with Chaos at the sisterhood, it was time for Lindsey to enjoy spending time with her friends without worrying about the world being taken over. After Lindsey had trapped Chaos in her vine attack and destroyed the necklace that controlled Cir's parents, they immediately had gone back to normal.

Cir's parents took some time taking in the sisterhood's air again after being trapped in despair with Chaos for so long before they assisted Lindsey. Together, Lindsey and Cir's parents, mainly Cir's parents, used a powerful spell to take away Chaos' power. After they had gotten trapped in the portal with Chaos, they had used their powerful minds to continue practicing magic.

Cir's parents sent Chaos to another dimension, a dimension that he could never come out of to hurt anyone ever again, and they found Serenity and stripped her of her powers as well. Cir assisted her parents in erasing Serenity's memory because the young girl didn't deserve the same fate as Chaos. After all, was said and done, the two reunited with their daughter and the moment the three of them shared was touching.

"Come on Lindsey, it's your turn," Laurie said when she noticed that Lindsey's mind was in space.

"Oh! Sorry!" Lindsey said and played her card. Even though Chaos would no longer be able to harm anyone, the sisterhood made a pact to protect the world from evil. Even though it was a team effort, the sisterhood honored Lindsey for fulfilling the prophecy. Even though she had helped, Lindsey was the witch who ultimately had defeated Chaos. However, when she looked at Laurie and Cir, she knew that wasn't true. They all had defeated Chaos, just as Lindsey had predicted.

When Lindsey put her mind to it, she was able to free Cir's parents from Chaos' control, so now Cir and her family could live happily ever after. No more living at the sisterhood's headquarters. Cir went home every night to loving parents who enrolled her in a human school.

"Draw four, Lindsey," Cir said happily.

"Oh man," Lindsey said as she gathered more cards into her already full hand. I need to pay more attention, Lindsey thought to herself.

And with that final thought, the three best friends, who

were also three powerful witches, yet still, three young girls finished their card game.

Fin

CHARLIE

BOOK

Made in the USA
Lexington, KY
19 June 2019